MURDER AT MIRROR LAKE

A Jillian Bradley
Mystery

Book 9

NANCY JILL THAMES

Murder at Mirror Lake

Cover by LLewellen Designs www.lyndseylewellen.wordpress.com
Photo credits:
Woman in green/ Zdenka Darula
Dreamstime.com
Beautiful grill place in autumn colors/Piotr Wawrzyniuk
Dreamstime.com
Adirondack chairs at lake shore/ Elena Elisseeva
Dreamstime.com
Yorkie Copyright: Scorpp/shutterstock.com
Author photo: Glamour Shots Barton Creek
Yorkshire terrier: "*Romeo*" Courtesy: Dan & Sara Olla
ISBN-10: 1499560818
ISBN-13: 978-1499560817
Category: *Fiction/Mystery &Detective/ Women Sleuths/Inspirational Fiction*

ACKNOWLEDGEMENTS

This book could only have been possible with the help of my Beta Reader Team and the tireless coaching from Brenda Burke Johnson. A heartfelt thank you goes Roxanne Day, Sid Frost, Karen Timmermann, Barbara Babcock, Deborah Fox Belisario, Maxine Rohde, and Gale O'Brien. A special thanks goes to my wonderful husband, Ted, who helped create the story and patiently listened to me talk about the work every day until launched, and to The Lord who is my inspiration for life.

PROLOGUE

When you are a senior citizen old enough for Medicare, change is often difficult. After living in a spacious two-story Victorian for years, I was still trying to get used to living in the renovated worker's cottage on the back of my property. Not that it was unpleasant. The smaller space was far cozier, and finding things was much easier than running up and down the stairs in my other house, looking for whatever I misplaced.

As I relaxed in my favorite leather recliner with a nice cup of tea and my Yorkie companion, Teddy, cuddled in my lap, I reminisced, as people my age often do.

Years had passed since my first husband died a hero in the Vietnam War, and until recently, my life was making sense, writing the "Ask Jillian" gardening column for *The San Francisco Enterprise* and its subsidiaries.

There was that and the occasional murder case I found myself involved in due to sheer happenstance. Those investigations created excitement, I have to admit.

I also recently married a wonderful man, an art dealer from my hometown, but he was killed right after our wedding had taken place in London. His death was devastating.

It was a marriage of convenience. Prentice Duvall and I were both lonely, loved fine art, and enjoyed each other's company.

Before he proposed, however, a botanist I'd been fond of a few years ago by the name of Dr. Vincent Fontaine tried to rekindle our old relationship. He concluded I'd be better off with the art dealer.

It was a mistake. I should have married the botanist.

After helping solve Prentice's case, I returned from London to Clover Hills and realized it was time for a new chapter in my life.

I made the decision to downsize, turning the worker's cottage on the back of my property into a cozy retreat, and inviting my favorite little family, the Montoyas, to live in the big house.

With them close, the loneliness was not as debilitating. Not being around reminders of my late husband, Prentice, was also less painful.

Sitting alone in my cottage, I finished my tea and contemplated my situation – I was widowed but healthy, childless but did have a darling godson named D. J. living in the big house, and I was well provided for thanks to The Lord and royalties from my column.

Teddy stretched in my lap and hopped down to the floor. He scurried to the kitchen, reminding me it was time for his dinner – and mine.

Satisfied with our meals, I tidied up the dishes, locked the doors, and headed for bed.

I needed a good night's sleep. tomorrow I would have to face my friends.

CHAPTER ONE

It was Ann Fielding's turn to host the Garden Club this month. Ann was my best friend and a woman I much admired. Not only was she a beautiful, sophisticated brunette, towering above my 5' 3" frame, Ann was a world traveler with a master's degree in French.

In a way, I dreaded our time together for fear she and my other garden club friends would ask about my recent trip to Costa Rica to visit the botanist I should have married.

It wasn't that the trip turned out badly – the visit was quite enjoyable, except for the uncomfortable way we parted.

I heaved a long sigh and cast a loving glance at Teddy, the little brown fur ball with blond highlights sitting at my feet. He cocked his head and yipped at the set of keys jingling in my hand.

"Yes, sweet doggie. You're coming with me to Ann's. I know you're excited. I'll let you outside in the yard for a minute. After you've finished, I'll get your leash and we'll be ready to go."

Teddy wagged his tail and panted at the mention of the word "go." It was one of his favorite words along with "walk," "fetch," and "dinner."

After buckling him safely in his special car seat, we headed to Ann's house through the golden, rolling hills of the Bay Area. Though the hills were referred to as "golden" because of the

1849 Gold Rush, I always thought of them as golden due to the dead grass.

When we arrived, I noticed other garden club members' cars parked in front. It appeared Nicole King and Dominique Summers were early.

Or was I late?

"Come on, Teddy. Let me get you out of your seat and get your leash on." I attached his red-rhinestone leash, which looked a little worn, to his collar, picked him up gently and made our way to the front door, and knocked.

"We must buy you a new leash. I can't have you looking neglected in front of my friends." How nice, I thought, to be able to shop for one online.

Within seconds, Ann answered the door wearing a turquoise sleeveless blouse and a pair of dressy white slacks. As always, she looked stunning.

Turquoise was her favorite color. Second only to purple, most of her clothes were turquoise. Even the walls in her family room were painted in her favorite color.

"Jillian!" She gave me a hug and peck on the cheek.

"Good to see you, Ann. I Hope you don't mind Teddy coming with me."

"Not at all. Teddy is always welcome. Come in." She gently scratched his ear. "Hi, little cutie."

With Teddy's leash and my purse added to the others on the entry bench, he rushed into the other room to greet the other ladies. I glanced around at Ann's lovely home and admired the magnificent view of her backyard filled with summer blooming shrubs and towering redwood trees, which bordered along the rear fence.

We'd been friends for so many years. I still remember when Ann first planted them. Yes, a walk around the grounds was definitely in order before I had to face the others.

Nicole smiled as I entered the family room. "Jillian, it's good to see you again." She was the savvy financial advisor of our group. We looked as different as night and day – she with her beautiful, long black tresses and me with my shoulder length blonde hair.

"How was your trip?" she asked.

A typical question I would ask someone. Why did I hedge?

"I had a good time. Thanks for asking. How's your family?" Would she notice my avoiding the subject?

Diminutive Dominique, ever the shy one, hugged me gently. "It's been a long time since I've seen you," she said as she searched me with her large brown eyes. "You've been to Costa Rica, I hear."

It was no use. My friends would not rest until I told them about going to see my old flame, Vincent Fontaine. Perhaps I'd throw them a bone for distraction.

"Before Jillian tells us *all* about her trip, let's have a walk in the garden," Ann said. "Afterward, we'll have tea."

Good. A reprieve. Time to think of unimportant but placating details to keep my friends from knowing the truth about what had happened. Why was I so worried? Even I didn't know what Vincent meant by what he said.

The garden was exquisite with deep blue morning glories climbing along the fence, rich magenta bougainvillea trellised on the deck wall, and a contemporary fountain bubbling in the middle of the courtyard in the side yard.

Ann was an accomplished gardener as well as a host extraordinaire.

The table was beautifully set for tea with ivory linens, a bouquet of lilacs, and "Old Country Roses" china Ann inherited from her mother. It was sad her mom died at such an early age from bone cancer. They were close. Since I was eight years older than Ann was, she often regarded me as a mother figure, which I didn't mind at all.

After we took our places at her lovely table, Ann offered milk for our tea, poured out, and stirred in sugar for those like me who insisted on sweetness.

"I'm serving your favorite mix of Darjeeling and Earl Grey in honor of your return trip, Jillian."

"How nice. Thank you. I'm convinced it tastes like the tea we had in London."

I swallowed hard, remembering the good times. And the bad.

Teddy patiently waited at my feet for any morsels I might choose to share. He was an intelligent little thing, especially when it came to making his desires understood. His nose twitched as he sniffed the air for possibilities.

The tea fare was delicious. Ann chose to serve quiche Florentine, a pear and gorgonzola salad with champagne vinaigrette, and fresh fruit compotes rimmed with green sugar. It was a lovely touch.

"We can't wait any longer, Jillian. Tell us about Costa Rica," Ann said.

The others chuckled.

I took a long sip of tea and offered Teddy a bite of quiche.

He almost bit my hand off. Maybe I didn't feed him enough breakfast this morning,

"I'm sorry, Ann. You were saying?"

The women stared at me, astonished!

I cleared my throat. "Costa Rica was beautiful. I stayed with Vincent's friends who were gracious, and we had an enjoyable time together. He showed me all over the country including the botanical research facility where he works at the university. You know how much he's into orchids."

My friends looked serious. They must have known something had happened between Vincent and me.

"So, what happened?" Nicole asked.

I took a deep breath. "I'm not really sure. On the way to the airport as I left, Vincent admitted he wasn't going to marry me."

Gasps all around the table.

Dominique scrunched her face. "*Wasn't* going to marry you or *couldn't* marry you, Jillian?"

"He may have said couldn't, but all I heard was the 'wasn't' part."

I broke down, laid my napkin on the table, and scooped Teddy up into my arms. "I'm sorry. Excuse me for a moment, please."

My friends sat stunned, but only for a few moments until they followed me into the living room.

I sat on the curved white sofa trying not to cry. "I'm sorry to have ruined your tea, Ann. It wasn't fair after all the trouble you went through."

She put her arm around my shoulder, and gently stroked Teddy. "I'm sure Vincent had a good reason for saying he can't marry you."

"If what you say is true, why didn't he tell me what it was? It's as if he doesn't trust my love for him enough to support him through something awful. I'm sorry. I didn't want to tell you at first, but now I'm glad to get it out."

Nicole hugged me. "We love you, Jillian."

"We're your friends and we care about you," Dominique said.

She had a point.

I caught Nicole whispering to Ann in a conspiratorial manner. What were they up to?

I remembered when I had met each one. Ann, a full time mom, playing with her son as I sat in the neighborhood park resting from taking Teddy on a walk. Striking up friendships with Nicole and Dominique working together on a committee for a neighborhood event.

Our group clicked once we found out how much each of us enjoyed gardening. Soon after, we formed our Garden Club – an excuse to meet once a month for lunch and take in each others' gardening endeavors.

Teddy licked my hand as if trying to console me.

I smiled at him, and looked at my dear friends. "Thank you, ladies. Your friendship over the years is precious. I'm sure I'll get over this disappointment, but after all I have been through, it hurts."

"We can understand," Nicole said. "You've suffered from the loss of two husbands."

"Thanks, Nicole. Losing one in Vietnam was bad enough, but losing Prentice at our reception was horrible. Oh dear, listen to me discussing unpleasant subjects at tea. I should be ashamed!"

"It's okay, Jillian," Ann said. "Speaking of which, if we're finished, I think it's time for the surprise."

Aha! It was close to my birthday, there might be a birthday cake. Any nice surprise in my life at this point would be welcome.

We gathered once again around the table and continued with our tea. The conversation turned to their children finding careers, working on graduate degrees, and hopes that finding mates in the near future would bring the promise of grandchildren.

"Refills?" Ann asked. She poured more steaming tea into my cup.

"How's the godson, D.J., doing these days?" Dominique sipped her tea. "He's almost two isn't he?"

I swallowed a bite of quiche before I replied. "We celebrated his second birthday last December at my house...or rather, at Walter and Cecilia's."

"Oh, right." Nicole used her napkin to wipe the corner of her mouth. "How do you like living in your new cottage? It was the old worker's house you renovated on the back of your property, wasn't it?"

"Actually, I like the coziness of the smaller space. It's much easier to keep. But the best part of the move is I'm frequently a dinner guest in my old kitchen with Walter and Cecilia. She loves to cook, and with me entertaining D.J. while she whips up a meal is a win-win situation for both of us. Cooking for one grew tiresome after so many years."

"I'm sure we'll all eventually reach that point." Nicole was being kind as usual.

As we finished eating, Dominique began clearing away dishes. "I can't wait for Jillian to hear about the surprise."

Nicole smiled. "Ann, may I help you with dessert?"

"Sure, I could use an extra set of hands."

All three of my friends sang me *Happy Birthday* as Nicole carried in the fresh strawberry cake lit with a single candle.

I was touched. "Oh, thank you!"

Teddy yipped as if he expected me to give him a morsel, which made my friends chuckle.

"Make a wish, Jillian," Ann said.

I closed my eyes, made a special wish to find the truth about Vincent, and blew out the candle.

"Ann, this cake is delicious." I took another forkful of yellow butter cake frosted with whipped cream and strawberries. It tasted especially good with the tea.

"I'll clean up later," Ann said. "Let's all go into the living room for the surprise."

My curiosity was peaked! I took a seat on the sofa and held Teddy in my lap.

"What have you ladies been up to?" I asked. No visible birthday presents anywhere.

Ann began. "The last time we met, you were in Costa Rica. We talked about many things but one thing in particular stayed with us."

"We think we should take a girl's getaway at least once before we're too far over the hill," Nicole said.

Dominique sat back and crossed her legs.

"You've mentioned on more than one occasion how much you'd love to see New England in the fall, Jillian," Ann said.

"I've always dreamed of going to upstate New York. I've heard raves from people who've been there."

"So if you'd like to join Nicole and me...."

"Unfortunately I'm on a buying trip to Zambia when they plan to go." Dominique was a buyer for African art from her home country.

"We've planned a trip for the three of us!" Ann said.

Words wouldn't come. After a moment, I said, "What a perfectly awesome idea!"

"Oh, good!" Ann said.

"I knew you'd like the idea." Nicole hugged me.

"This is quite a birthday gift!" I was kidding, of course. "I don't mind paying my own way."

Nicole and Ann smiled at each other.

"It's only part of the surprise." Dominique uncrossed and crossed her legs again. "Why don't you tell her the best part, Ann?"

Ann finished a bite of cake. "When I checked for tours and accommodations, there weren't many venues who took dogs. Not even thinking about it, I found a photo of this charming colonial inn and called. The place sounded perfect until I mentioned Teddy."

Nicole chimed in.

"Before Ann ended the call, the woman handling the reservations suddenly recognized who we were from our first murder incident in Half Moon Bay years ago."

"Who was she?" I asked.

"Do you remember Ingrid Sorenson?" Ann asked.

I racked my brain.

"The woman who headed the master gardener program at LaBelles Nursery in Canyon Grove?" I leaned forward.

Teddy jumped off my lap, positioned himself at my feet, ears cocked, and waited for a morsel of cake.

I slipped him a tiny bite of strawberries and whipped cream, which he accepted gratefully with a wag of his tail.

"The same one," Ann said. "When I mentioned your name and explained about Teddy, she graciously offered to let you stay in her cottage on the property. I told her we'd do our best to convince you."

"Of course, Ann and I will stay at the inn. We reserved a suite overlooking Mirror Lake."

"Mirror Lake?" I sat up. "That's where we're going? Isn't it near Lake Placid where the winter Olympics was held?"

Dominique quickly checked Google for the information. "The one in 1932 and in 1980."

"So you're in, Jillian?" Ann nodded.

"I would love to see Ingrid again. What's she doing in Lake Placid?"

Nicole accepted another refill from Ann, and spoke.

"After her husband passed away, her daughter, Claire, I think her name is, insisted she move closer to her. Claire is a host for a restaurant at the Mirror Lake Inn and helped her mother find a desk clerk job when there was an opening. Ingrid's worked there three years now, she said."

"How does she like living in upstate New York?" I asked.

Ann shrugged. "She said she loves the Adirondacks and *most* of the people she works with."

Most was not lost on me.

Dominique furrowed her brow. "Didn't Claire get married around here somewhere? Was it at the Canyon Grove Country Club?"

"I remember attending her wedding," I said. "It was at Elliston Vineyards in Canyon Grove. A beautiful wedding, as I recall."

"How did Claire wind up in Lake Placid? A bit far from home, don't you think?" Nicole stood. "I need to leave soon for an appointment with a client."

Nicole was always busy with clients since she knew how to make profitable investments.

Ann stood, too, and gathered empty plates. "Ingrid mentioned something about Claire's husband, Sam. He's finishing his degree online and working part time at one of the inn's restaurants. Evidently, Sam is from the area. His father owns a local produce farm close by. Organic, I think she said."

"Organic seems to be the trend now." Dominique slipped the strap of her purse over her shoulder to leave.

"I visited Lake Placid once," she said. "Our son trained for the Ironman one summer. The area is much different from the Bay Area. More beautiful, I think. I remember the town being quaint with a touch of Sweden."

"It must have been the Olympic influence. Don't they call sites like Lake Placid 'Olympic villages?'"

Ann's comment triggered images in my mind of snow covered mountain chalets.

"Wait a minute." She took out her cell phone. "I have a picture of Mirror Lake Inn."

The hotel reminded me of the inn in the movie *White Christmas* with Bing Crosby and Danny Kaye. "How lovely. The structure looks old, typical of the region from what people have said about the area. I wonder if it's owned by a chain."

Nicole hugged us. "I really need to run. And by the way, the inn is family owned. It was built in 1924. I read the history on their website."

"Interesting." I wondered if Ingrid's comment referred to one of the family.

Teddy started for the front door.

"Woof!" He barked.

I shook my head. "I think he's trying to tell me it's time to get home. Traffic will be heavy at this time of day. Ann, thank you for the tea party and birthday cake. You ladies have brightened my spirits. I'm grateful.

I secured Teddy's leash. "By the way, when is the trip?"

"We leave mid-September." Ann handed me my purse. "I was told it's the peak season for leaf peepers."

"Leaf peepers?" I asked.

She smiled. "That's what they call us."

"I can't wait!"

For some reason the term 'peepers' made me think of the song, "Jeepers, Creepers," and the recollection of a horror movie by the name of "Lake Placid" entered my mind.

I shuddered.

CHAPTER TWO

The morning of our trip finally arrived. After packing for myself, I went to the freezer and took out a week's worth of homemade frozen dinner packets for Teddy. Ground turkey or hamburger mixed with mixed vegetables ready for the microwave.

"Let me see – a package of shredded cheese, fruit cups, and individual servings of brown and wild rice for a well-rounded meal. I believe I have everything." I tucked the items into a small ice-chest filled with bags of ice.

"Woof!" Teddy barked.

"Oh sorry. You'll want doggie treats, too."

He wagged his tail as I reached in the cupboard and took out the box of his favorites.

"Now we're ready, little one."

I hired a shuttle to take Teddy and me to the airport. Our flight would arrive in Albany late afternoon where we would rent a car and drive to Lake Placid, hopefully in time for dinner at the inn.

Since it was such a long trip, we decided to take the shortest flight time wise, even though it stopped once.

"Whoever suggested going first class was smart." I nodded to Ann seated next to the window.

She smiled in agreement.

"Lake Placid, here we come," Nicole said.

With Teddy in his case tucked under the seat in front, I stretched out in the oversized leather recliner and buckled my seatbelt. I loved the special attention and warm mixed nuts.

By the time we arrived, I was more than ready to stretch my legs in spite of the plush oversized seats and attentive service.

As usual, Teddy took the trip in stride like a champ. He was used to traveling with me, thank goodness, and slept almost the whole time except when I gave him ice to munch on so he wouldn't get too thirsty.

"I'll get the rental car," Ann said.

I knew she'd insist on a luxury SUV with good visibility and comfort for sightseeing.

"I'll watch for the bags," Nicole said.

"Come on, Teddy. Let's take you for a break in the dog area outside and find you a drink of water."

A slight breeze brushed past. The air was crisp and clean. Teddy sniffed trying to catch the scents of dogs who'd visited the site.

Once we claimed our bags and found the rental, we piled our stuff in the back of the large white SUV and studied our surroundings. The whole area was ablaze with color! I placed Teddy on his towel next to me on the back seat.

"The leaves are breathtaking!" Nicole said.

"We made it!" Ann buckled her seat belt and set a course on her phone to the Mirror Lake Inn. "We should be there in a couple of hours or so."

Nicole sat in front with Ann. "I think we can hold out for dinner after all the food they served on our flight."

"I agree," I said. Teddy would be fine with the snacks I brought.

Our adventure as leaf peepers had begun!

Thank you, Lord for a safe trip so far.

As we approached the lonelier stretch of highway outside of Albany toward the Adirondacks, the Ausable River came into view as if escorting us on our way to Lake Placid. It skipped merrily, twisting and turning over rocks, bubbling along as we drove through magnificent forests interspersed with deciduous trees, putting on a show of radiant colors in bright orange, deep yellow and cherry red.

Mountains loomed ahead with rising mists of fog at their bases. At one point Ann had to turn on the windshield wipers to get rid of the moisture.

"Look," she said. "We're coming into Keene Valley. You can see Adirondack chairs now."

She was right. The distinctive wood slat chairs were in the front yards, on porches, and for sale in country stores. We were close.

"We're not too far, now." Nicole referred to her phone's map app. She stretched her neck toward her window and looked out. "We're here! There's the ski jump on our left."

Rising high in the air, the several stories tall ski jump towered over the town coming into view.

"Lake Placid is directly ahead." Ann nodded.

We passed the United States Training Center, Olympic Center, and other buildings built just for the Olympics. During snow season, people came from all over the world to enjoy winter sports in this picturesque town. In summer, I read Mirror Lake was the site for the Iron Man competition.

"Drive slowly, Ann," I said. "I want to take in Main Street. Look how quaint it is." Charming restaurants and specialty stores lined the street. "Let's have lunch and do some shopping one day while we're here."

"I'm for that." Ann slowed her speed.

When I saw all the art galleries and gift shops, I knew we had come to the right place for our getaway. A twinge of remorse hit me, though, when I realized my art collecting days were probably at an end.

The walls of the house I bequeathed to Walter and Cecilia were covered with works I'd collected over the years. When I moved into the cottage, I went with a beach theme to display my shell collection, and only moved a couple of my favorite works to my new abode.

We had come to Mirror Lake Drive. The Mirror Lake Inn loomed on the left, a white colonial hotel several stories high perched across the street from the lake. On the right was The Cottage, a small eatery with a rainbow of umbrellas on the patio.

"It looks inviting, doesn't it?" Nicole said.

Ann nodded ahead. "Look at the little two story lake cottage next to it. It has a wraparound porch complete with rocking chairs."

She drove into the back lot and found a place to park.

We were ready to stretch our legs.

I motioned to what appeared to be the back entry. "I think you can go in there."

I secured Teddy with his leash and set him on the pavement. He stretched his paws out in front and sniffed the air.

"Ladies, go on in and check into your room. I'll text Ingrid and let her know Teddy and I have arrived."

Ann tossed me the car key. "I'll leave the car open so we can get our bags. You may need to use it to get your things to Ingrid's cottage."

"Good thinking, Ann. Why don't we meet for dinner after we've settled in?"

Nicole nodded. "Send us a text when you're ready."

The grounds were impeccable with baskets of colorful petunias and greenery dotting the landscape. In the distance, a fog bank shrouded the mountains overlooking the lake. It was as if something was hidden from me. I was reminded of Vincent's decision not to marry me. What was he hiding?

A text vibrated on my phone. Ingrid was answering my message:

I'll be there in two minutes, Jillian. I have a car to take your things.

So I wouldn't need the key.

Ingrid pulled up, and greeted me. She hadn't changed since I saw her last. Happy face, plump bosom, and same short brown hairstyle, practical for working in her garden.

"I'm thrilled you could come, Jillian. Let me help you get your luggage."

"That would be wonderful. It's good to see you again. I can't thank you enough for letting Teddy and me stay with you. It's very generous."
She cast a glance at Teddy. "He's adorable. May I pick him up?"
"He would love the attention. He usually does. Teddy, this is Ingrid. She'd like to hold you."
Teddy yipped as if to say, "I'd like that."
She reached down and picked him up, snuggling him to her chest. "What a sweetie! I may just keep you, little one."
I shook my head. "I don't know if I could do without him. However, I might let you dog sit if the need arises."
"I'd love to. Now let's be on our way. I can't wait for you to see my cottage, especially my garden."
We drove through the parking lot and down a small side road only a little ways from the inn and pulled up in front of a small white cottage built in the same colonial style as the hotel.
The front yard was garden – every square inch!
"Ingrid, this is amazing. Your master gardener experience shows."
She smiled. "Thanks. I'll show you to your room."
She helped carry in the bags while I carried in Teddy with all his paraphernalia. Tote, monogram blue towel that my godson D.J.'s other grandma had given me for a wedding present, and insulated lunch container, filled with his food.
"Woof!" he said as I set him on the floor.

"I think Teddy is asking for a bowl of water," I said. "I brought his bowl and feeding dish."

"So he lets you know what he wants."

"The dog is uncanny."

"Good to know. The kitchen is over there." She nodded as she took the cooler. "I'll put his food in the fridge."

"Thanks."

"There's only one bathroom, I'm afraid. I hope you don't mind sharing."

I chuckled.

"Not at all. When I was growing up, our family of six shared a single bathroom with only one sink. You should have seen us on Sunday mornings getting ready for church!"

Bells began to peal. It was almost as if I had triggered them by my last comment.

"Those are the bells from St. Eustace Episcopal Church in the Village of Lake Placid." Ingrid said.

"They're beautiful."

Teddy pricked up his ears with each ring. He cocked his head as if trying to discern where the sounds were coming from.

Ingrid started from the room.

"I need to tell Claire you're here. She wanted to make special dinner reservations for you and your friends. I'm off for the evening, so I can stay with Teddy if you like."

A qualm of uneasiness washed over me at her suggestion. It was from the time I'd almost lost him in Half Moon Bay when I left him alone in my hotel room. I vowed never to leave him alone or with anyone I didn't trust.

It was silly not to trust Ingrid. We had been friends for a long time, even though it was quite a while since we talked.

"You mustn't worry about him, Jillian. I heard about what happened in Half Moon Bay. Show me what to give him to eat and I promise we'll stay here. I'll keep him company until you get back."

"Okay. Thank you. I'll take him for a quick trip outside before I leave."

"Should I tell her six o'clock or seven?"

"I think six o'clock will suit everyone."

The sun was starting to set as I walked the short distance to the inn to meet my friends for dinner.

A few people walked along the roads and sidewalks in different directions, some walked dogs. I wondered where they lived since guests were not allowed to bring pets.

Near the back entrance, I noticed a note of congratulations painted on the adjoining wall. It was to Drew Olson for his Olympic medal.

Impressive.

Once inside, I walked down the narrow hall which came out into the main living room area.

A guest sat near the fire reading a book. She looked comfortable.

Ann and Nicole could wait until I'd looked around a bit since I was early.

I strolled into the library on the other side of the fireplace into a sitting area with tan leather sofas and chairs placed around a square mahogany coffee table.

Over the mantle, a giant moose head caught my eye. Adirondack themed pillows and accessories decorated the mahogany walled room.

After perusing the bookshelves, I sat down on a sofa facing the fire.

A young woman stepped in and smiled. "Are you Jillian Bradley?"

"Yes. You must be Claire." She favored her mother except for the soft wavy brown hair worn to her shoulders.

She extended her hand. "Claire Hunt. It's nice to see you again. Mom said you were at my wedding but that day was such a blur I don't remember anyone except Sam."

"That's understandable. Your wedding was lovely."

A smile crossed her pixie-like face in the shape of a heart.

"I came to tell you your friends are waiting to be seated. I don't think they saw you in here."

"I'd better join them."

I followed her a little way past the stairs leading down to the main entry. A beautiful crystal chandelier hung over the stairwell.

"The spa is downstairs," she said.

Ann and Nicole came out from the *Taste Bistro Bar* where they had been waiting.

"Sorry to keep you but I had to have a look around at this remarkable hotel," I said.

"Wait until you see our suite," Nicole said. "After dinner, we'll take you up. It's on the next floor."

Claire motioned for us to follow. "This way, ladies. I've saved you seats with a view of the lake."

She led us to a small table covered with a white tablecloth, set with fresh flowers. A flickering candle added an elegant touch. The view was stunning!

"You're welcome to look at the menu." She handed each of us one. "But I've taken the liberty of asking Chef Gumm to prepare something special for you tonight."

We looked appreciatively at each other.

"When Mom told our manager Jillian Bradley was coming, he insisted on giving you special treatment. Evidently he's a fan of the *Ask Jillian Column*."

"You're a celebrity, Jillian," Ann said.

I blushed. "I'm honored. Please thank him for me."

Claire looked over her shoulder at a rather formidable looking man with graying temples approaching. "You can thank him yourself."

"Good evening, ladies," he said. "Drew Olson, general manager at your service. We're delighted to have you stay with us. How are your rooms?"

Ann put her menu down. "Comfortable. Thank you."

"The CD playing was a nice touch. Especially after a travel day." Nicole turned toward me as if it was my turn to say something.

"I'm Jillian Bradley. I'm staying with Ingrid since pets aren't allowed here."

"Your photo doesn't do you justice!"

"Yes...Ingrid mentioned you read my column."

"I apologize, ma'am for not allowing pets. Those have been the rules since we opened in 1924."

He turned and glanced toward the front desk. "If you'll excuse me, I think Chef Gumm is approaching to tell you about his offerings tonight. Again, it's a pleasure to have you as our guests."

Chef Gumm stepped forward dressed in a double-breasted white smock and tall chef's hat.

"Good evening. I hope you'll enjoy what I've prepared for you tonight."

I was so tired I could have eaten a bowl of soup and a roll and been happy.

From the looks of Chef Gumm, I had an idea the food would be on the rich side. He was stocky and wore a short dark beard reminding me of Bluto in the Popeye cartoons.

A pair of gold-rimmed half-reading glasses hung on a chain around his neck. He spoke with a European accent.

"To start, we have a Harmony Hills pork pâté, served with salted pretzel, house-made mustard, cornichons, and shallot jam. This will be followed by our parmesan custard Caesar salad with house-made lemon Caesar dressing, hearts of romaine, marinated white anchovies, rustic herb croutons, parmesan custard, and preserved lemon.

Ann raised her eyebrows as if impressed.

"For the main course, I'll be serving my specialty free-range chicken breast stuffed with Hudson Valley foie gras and fines herbes, pan roasted pommes puree, mustard greens, figs, and sherry pan jus."

Chef Gumm looked pleased with himself. "We proudly served locally grown produce from Hunt's Produce Farm."

I took note of the name – it was the same as Claire's.

"And for dessert...a red raspberry crème brûlée served with salted chocolate tuile and fresh berries."

My mouth began to water.

The chef rubbed his hands together. "Now if you'll excuse me, I'll have your appetizer served."

"Wow," Nicole said. "I bet this meal will be close to $100 apiece." As a financial planner, she probably read the menu prices and added his suggestions up in her head.

"Oh well, I'm sure it will be worth it," Ann said. "Look at this view!"

Two storied picture windows framed in mahogany looked out onto the lake surrounded by tall pines. A man in a canoe rowed past and out of sight. To add to the ambiance, a fire burned as we ate and watched the sunset shining on the water.

After we managed to get through the rich food, with me only eating half portions as my secret weapon to keep my weight down, Claire brought us cappuccinos.

"Compliments of the house."

She handed me a small sack. "Chef Gumm heard you brought Teddy. He loves dogs and thought Teddy would enjoy these scraps."

"Thank him for me. The dinner was wonderful. I think we all appreciated it."

Ann and Nicole thanked her as well.

"Do you have time to see our suite?" Nicole asked.

I peered outside. "I think I'll walk back while it's still light." I handed Ann the keys back. "Why don't we meet after breakfast? I'll see it then."

"Goodnight, Jillian," Ann said.

"Night."

As I started back, I thought about what Ann had mentioned as we planned the trip. Ingrid said she gets along with most people she works with here. So far, I'd met the head chef and the hotel manager. Neither raised any concerns. And yet something felt wrong.

Who were the others?

CHAPTER THREE

Darkness had fallen by the time I reached Ingrid's cottage. The walk after dinner might not have been such a good idea. After a long day of travel, I was almost asleep on my feet. Upon reaching her front door, I could hear Teddy's yips from within.

Ingrid stood in the doorway holding him.

Teddy wriggled and wagged his tail, excited to see his "mommy."

I took him in my arms and kissed the top of his head. "Were you a good boy?"

Ingrid closed the door and offered me a seat on the chintz sofa. "He's been a little doll. How was your dinner?"

As we chatted, I stroked Teddy gently.

"We received the royal treatment from your sweet daughter. She had Chef Gumm come to our table to tell us about the food.

"The chicken breast stuffed with foie gras was amazing, not to mention the succulent raspberry crème brûlée. Such flavor! The general manager...."

"Drew Olson?"

"Yes, I believe that was his name. Anyway he was very very gracious and wanted to make sure we were totally satisfied."

"Drew reads your column."

I nodded. "He told me at dinner."

"Gardening is his hobby. I think it's one of the reasons he hired me."

"*Your* garden is incredible. I'm looking forward to admiring it when I get the chance."

She rose and turned to me. "Can I get you anything before you go to bed?"

I chuckled. "I am exhausted. Does it show?"

Ingrid smiled.

"Caught me. When guests come to the inn, I can tell which ones are tired. Usually the kids are the ones bursting with energy."

"I think what I need is a cup of herbal tea and a nice hot soak in the tub. I brought my own bubble bath.

She shook her head. "You're too much, Jillian. I'll be right back with your tea. Milk? Sugar? It's chamomile."

"Three sugars, please. And no milk. Thanks."

"Three?" she asked.

"I think I must be part ant."

Ingrid headed for the kitchen while I carried Teddy into the guest room to unpack.

He hopped down and started to sniff every nook and cranny of our lodgings.

The room was lovely. Blush pink walls set off the white open beamed ceiling. Next to the black iron bed, Ingrid had made the room welcoming with a fresh bouquet in a blue, spatter painted pitcher on top of a small dresser. I recognized the flowers from her garden. Above the dresser hung a hand-painted mirror.

After I set my suitcase on top of the bed, I placed the blue towel at the foot and unpacked.

"Knock, knock," Ingrid said. "Here's your tea. I'll just set it on the dresser and you can drink it whenever you like."

"Thanks."

"Can I get you anything else before I head to bed?"

"No, I'm going to bed myself."

She gave Teddy a pat and wished us goodnight.

Teddy looked exhausted.

"It's time you went to sleep, precious pup. There will be plenty of exploring tomorrow."

When I put him on his towel, he stretched and circled around until he was comfortable. Satisfied, he lay down and closed his eyes.

The soothing tea and bubble bath worked their magic. A spritz of perfume to enhance good dreams and I was ready for bed.

Before I slipped beneath the covers, I went to the window. Outside, pine branches swayed softly as I looked out over the lake. Moonlight on the water reflected mountains shrouded in fog. Along the shore, specks of light glinted from dense patches of trees and foliage.

All was quiet.

Thank you, Lord for a safe trip so far. Amen.

With a tiny lick on my cheek the next morning, Teddy awakened me. When I opened my eyes, his little face greeted me with a look of "I need to go outside."

"Okay, boy. Let me get dressed and I'll take you for a...." I caught myself before mentioning the word "walk" to avoid his barking and possibly waking Ingrid.

Teddy was extremely intelligent. I truly believed he understood most things I said.

I slipped on a pair of jeans, a black checked shirt, and a cable knit sweater, the color of grapes.

Ingrid was nowhere in sight. I went to the kitchen and found a note to help myself to breakfast if I wished.

A coffee cake beckoned on the counter. It looked delicious. Teddy's nose began to sniff the air.

"Come on, Teddy. Let's put on your leash and I'll take you outside. I promise I'll give you a bite when we get back."

Ingrid was busy weeding in the front yard.

"So there you are," I said.

"Good morning, Jillian. I like to fuss with my garden before I start my shift. It puts me in a good frame of mind."

"That makes sense. Weeding, I see."

She stood straight and caught her breath.

"As you probably know, the weeding will give the nicotiana, poppies, and verbena bonariensis a better chance to shed their seeds. It gives them a head start in spring."

"Good tip. I need to walk Teddy, but I'll be back in a minute. Your coffee cake looks tempting."

She smiled. "I wish I could tell you I baked it but Chef Gumm insisted I take it home to share with you."

"He seems nice."

Ingrid paused. "He can be if you don't cross him."

Perhaps Chef Gumm was *not* included in her getting along with "most people" as first mentioned to Ann when the reservation was made.

Teddy and I started for our walk along a path toward the lake.

From out of nowhere, a black and tan dog rushed past.

Teddy yipped at the surprise visitor as I instinctively grabbed the dog's collar. It was a Schnauzer with a tan muzzle and long eyebrows to match. A woman with blonde hair followed the escapee.

"Fritz!" she said.

"Fritz cocked his ears and lowered his head, as if being caught doing something bad.

"Bad boy," the woman said. "Thanks for catching him." She caught her breath and extended her hand. "I'm Eva, Eva Gumm, Ingrid's neighbor."

"Hello. I'm Jillian Bradley and this is Teddy."

She let him smell her hand, and gave him a stroke.

"I'm sure Fritz just wanted to make Teddy's acquaintance."

Eva attached a leash to Fritz's harness. She rubbed his ears. "Schnauzers are noted for being headstrong. This one is active as you can see."

"You must be Chef Gumm's wife," I said.

"I am. When you have time, you and Teddy please drop by and have a cup of coffee. I'm home most of the time."

"Thank you. I will."

"I'd better toddle off. It's time for his training. We have an obstacle course set up behind our house. If I'm ever to get any peace, I have to wear him out first."

We both chuckled.

"Thanks for the coffee invitation."

"Come over anytime. We're next door." She pointed to a two-story home, much larger than Ingrid's.

We waved goodbye and Teddy and I returned home. The yard was empty. I assumed Ingrid was inside.

"I'm in the kitchen," she said as she stuck her head in the doorway. "Coffee?"

"Thanks."

"Teddy has fresh water."

"Thanks. I'll make his breakfast."

I took out ground turkey and fruit from the fridge and prepared a nice meal for him.

Teddy marched over to his feeding dish and ate every morsel I'd prepared. Afterward, he went to the water and lapped.

"How do you take your coffee?" she asked.

"Black, thanks."

I sat at the small table in front of a window overlooking the lake. The tablecloth looked vintage. So pretty.

She handed me a mug. "The cake is for anytime you want a piece."

"I don't think I can stand to wait any longer."

Ingrid smiled and served me a small slice. Teddy returned immediately to my side and looked up at me with his pleading little eyes.

"You can't still be hungry after you just ate your breakfast! Oh here you go." I offered him a tiny morsel.

She refilled my coffee, cut herself a piece of cake, and joined me at the table.

"We met Eva and Fritz a little while ago."

"Did he escape again?" She chuckled. "That dog is a handful. But they both love him. They tried to have children but were never successful."

"Eva seemed nice. She invited me for coffee."

"Eva? She is nice. Nicer than her husband, if you ask me."

"Why do you say that?"

Ingrid looked sheepish.

"I shouldn't say anything. Chef Gumm is difficult to please. I'll leave it at that."

"He's a chef. I would suspect creative types can be difficult at times."

"You might be right."

I eyed the cake.

"Would you care for another slice? The first one was small."

"Thanks. I'll walk it off somehow." I got up from my chair. "I'll get it."

She looked pleased.

"What are your plans today, Jillian?" She sipped her coffee and took a bite of coffee cake."

"Ann and Nicole have a trip planned I think. We've come to be leaf peepers."

She smiled at the term. "You'll get an eye full where ever you go. Upstate New York has gorgeous fall color."

After finishing the last bite of cake, she stood.

"I need to wash up and go to work. If you want, I can keep Teddy until after you talk with your friends. I have the mid-morning to late afternoon shift. I get off at four."

"That should be plenty of time. Thanks, Ingrid. He'll probably take a nap for most of the morning."

"After you leave, I'll put him on the sofa so he'll be able to see me."

"Well, Teddy, it looks as if you have a new sitter."

"Woof!" he barked.

The text from Ann read:

Our room number is 3705. Come on up when you get here.

The elevator took me to their room – a comfortable suite furnished with rustic mahogany four-poster beds and richly upholstered furniture.

"Wait right there," Nicole said. "I want you to listen to the CD. It creates one of the most relaxing atmospheres I've ever been in."

She turned on the CD player. I had to agree – the music relaxed me at once.

Ann hugged me. "Take a look the view from our balcony."

The pristine lake held a few swimmers and one or two boaters paddling around.

"Look at the color!" I said.

"The only thing I don't like about our room is the view of the dumpsters off our bedroom. I suppose no room is perfect."

"Have you two eaten?" I asked.

"We had the buffet downstairs. What about you, Jillian?" Ann asked.

"Ingrid fed me coffee cake. She's taking care of Teddy for me until we leave. What's the plan?"

Ann sat in the large wingback chair and put her feet up on the matching ottoman. "I ordered a picnic lunch to take along. The drive will take us to Whiteface Mountain, one of the high peaks of the Adirondack Mountains. On a clear day there's a 360 degree view of the Adirondacks and glimpses of Vermont."

"I read if the weather is clear enough, we may even see Canada. It's a pleasant drive up and back. The article also said the Green Mountains are visible from there," Nicole said.

"I'm ready whenever you are," I said.

Nicole turned off the CD and grabbed her purse.

Ann led the way to the car. "Let's grab Teddy and we'll be on our way."

Storm clouds moved in followed by the chiming of the bells.

We looked at each other. After being friends for so many years, we must have been thinking the same thing.

This does not look good.

CHAPTER FOUR

The storm was over by the time we reached the base of Whiteface Mountain. We drove five miles to reach the summit, parked, and stretched our legs. The air smelled fresh and sweet after the rain.

"I brought binoculars," Ann said. Of all my friends, she was the most prepared for any eventuality.

After letting Teddy on the ground to sniff his new environment, he hovered cautiously by my side.

Surrounded by forests in blazing colors of oranges and reds against the deep green pines, the views were spectacular.

"I'm glad we came," I said.

"Me, too," Nicole said. "Is anyone else hungry?"

"I'm always hungry," I said.

Ann agreed. "Find a spot and I'll bring the lunch."

Much to my friends' delight, we arrived back at the inn in time for tea. "Sorry you'll miss out," Nicole said.

"You ladies enjoy," I said. "I'll take Teddy to the cottage and rest a bit."

"We'll stay in touch," Ann said.

Before turning in to the gate of Ingrid's cottage, I noticed Eva sitting on her side lawn in a dark green Adirondack chair.

Fritz was lying beside her.

"Jillian, yoo-hoo!" Eva said. "How about a cup of coffee?"

I couldn't be rude.

"I'd love one," I said.

Teddy pricked up his ears when he saw Fritz.

"Woof!" he barked.

Eva held Fritz fast with his leash and shook her finger. "Not this time, you don't.

"Would you like to come inside or have coffee out here?"

The afternoon was so lovely and the other Adirondack chair seemed to beckon.

"Outside would be good."

"Fritz, stay with Teddy and I'll be right back." She turned to me. "You don't mind, do you?"

"Not at all."

Glad of the company, the dogs wrestled playfully.

Eva brought a tray with mugs of coffee and a plate of pastries. "Gumby made these this morning. I'm so lucky to have a chef for a husband."

There was a note of uncertainty in her voice. It could be my imagination or maybe Ingrid's words still hanging in the air.

"My life is lonely at times," Eva said. "His schedule keeps him late, often until 2 a.m. when he does the accounting."

"Such a schedule would be difficult to keep up with." I took a sip of coffee.

"What about you, Jillian. Are you married?"

"I was, twice. Both are dead."

"I'm sorry."

"My last husband and I were only married a few hours."

Eva leaned in. "Oh my goodness! What happened?"

"He was poisoned at our wedding reception. I don't like to talk about it."

"I can certainly understand."

My thoughts drifted a moment.

"It's funny – Prentice wanted our wedding to be so special. That's why he planned the destination wedding in London around one of his business trips."

"A horrible fate for him. What about children?"

"None, I'm afraid. All I have is a large extended family and a young couple I'm close to back home."

"Our family is small, too. It's only my brother and me since our mother passed away last year. He's the inn's general manager – Drew Olson."

"Really?"

"Mom lived in a nursing home in Lake Placid. She was a handful but I do miss her."

"Did she have Alzheimer's?"

"She must have been on the verge. Before she died, the caregivers tried to tell us she was more difficult to manage. We should have listened."

"Dealing with aging parents can be a challenge. My mother still lives independently, but the family has talked about care for her in the future."

"Drew was good about looking after her. He's still on the hospital board. We both took turns visiting her once a week."

I selected a pastry.

Teddy was immediately by my side.

"Woof!" he barked.

I pulled a tiny piece from the end and gave it to him.

"Sometimes I think he just wants to remind me he's here."

"What about dinner tonight? You'll probably want to eat with your friends."

"Yes. Ingrid offered to watch Teddy for me."

"Well, if she can't, please don't hesitate to ask me. Fritz loves the company."

"I'm relieved to hear you say that. It's gracious of you."

I looked at the time on my phone.

"I'd better go and get ready. Thanks for the coffee and pastry. I had better keep an eye on my weight while I'm here."

"You look great for your age."

I blushed. "Thanks."

"Come along, Teddy. We need to go."

Using Ingrid's house key, I made myself at home.

Trying to decide what to wear for dinner wasn't too difficult. The blue sheath had always been one of my favorites. I added a long string of black and crystal beads to complete the outfit and slipped on patent leather flats. I was almost ready to go.

"Anyone home?" Ingrid asked.

Teddy yipped.

"In the guest room, getting dressed."

After a quick spritz of perfume, I joined her in the living room.

"You look lovely, Jillian. Better be careful tonight."

I chuckled. "Right."

"You never know who'll be there. I've seen all kinds."

"Your job must be interesting serving guests from all over the country."

Ingrid plopped on the sofa. "It is. The only drawback is standing on my feet all day."

"Don't you take breaks?"

"A few in the kitchen. But there always seems to be friction so it doesn't feel like a break."

"The staff doesn't get along?"

She shook her head. "Most of us do."

"Chef Gumm? I assume that's who you're referring to as the irregular person."

She nodded.

"If he's so difficult, why doesn't the general manager replace him?"

"It's not so simple. From what I've learned, he wouldn't have anywhere else to go if he left the inn."

"I see. Something happened to make him a pariah."

"You're a good detective, Jillian. And Eva is Drew's sister."

"She shared that."

"Because of her, Drew won't fire him."

Chef Gumm's past was intriguing.

I set Teddy's supper out – cooked ground turkey, peas and carrots, and a spoonful of brown and wild rice mixture. I sprinkled on a bit of cheese and added a few pieces of fruit to make a delectable meal for my small companion.

With a clink, I set his bowl on the floor and Teddy wagged his tail in appreciation.

It was time to meet my friends for dinner.

Ingrid offered to give me a lift.

"I'll be okay. It's such a beautiful night and the walk will do me good. Thanks anyway."

After I slipped on my coat and grabbed my purse, I headed toward the inn.

Mirror Lake was magic. With such an array of tall trees standing hundreds of feet in the air and majestic mountains surrounding the water, I was captivated by the beautiful serenity of this place.

The inn at night shimmered with lights, reminding me of a fairyland. Ann and Nicole were waiting to greet me by the fire in the living room.

My friends looked stunning in their outfits – Ann, statuesque and sophisticated, and Nicole with her long dark hair reminiscent of an Indian princess.

I sat with them a moment.

"How was afternoon tea?" I asked.

"Extremely civilized," Nicole said. "The host served us whatever kind we liked."

"And they served all the chocolate chip cookies you could eat," Ann said.

"Where are we dining tonight?" I asked.

Ann nodded toward the bar. "I read great reviews for *Taste Bistro*. Why don't we try it?"

Claire was at her station taking reservations for *The View*. She gave a nod as we approached.

A young man behind the front desk said, "Good evening, ladies. Will you be joining us for dinner?"

"We're going to try *Taste Bistro*," Ann said.

"A good choice," he said. "Have a good evening."

"Thank you, John." I said.

Nicole seemed surprised.

"Do you know him?"

I chuckled.

"No. I read his name badge."

A friendly host seated us at a table overlooking the lake. The view was magnificent.

We sat near the fireplace with another moose head watching over the guests. The room was full of patrons, mostly our age, and a few young people sitting close to each other.

"We have to try the pot roast. I've read nothing but raves," Ann said.

The server took our orders, and returned with our drinks.

"...and a cranberry juice with a twist of lime on the rocks for you, ma'am."

"Thank you," I said.

In one corner of the room, a man sitting at a table with another gentleman smiled and raised his drink to me.

"Don't look, but I think the man in the brown jacket and glasses sitting in the corner is hitting on me."

Without being too conspicuous, Nicole stole a glance. "You're right. He's staring at you. What are you going to do?"

I sipped my juice. "Ignore him. If he knew how old I was, he'd quit with such nonsense."

We enjoyed a chuckle.

A guitarist entered and began playing soft jazz, adding to the ambiance.

Nicole ordered the cheese platter appetizer – perfect to dispel hunger pangs.

I glanced out of the corner of my eye at the man who flirted with me.

He'd turned to face the man he was with and was now bent in conversation. Serious by the look of it.

The server arrived with the steaming pot roast and savory caramelized vegetables. The meat melted in my mouth.

Teddy would appreciate a doggie bag from this meal.

With no one waiting for a table, we felt comfortable to stay and listen to the guitarist play as long as we wanted.

Most of the other guests seemed to be enjoying him as much as we were. Even the men at the table in the corner were listening to him play.

Ann stifled a yawn. "I'm feeling all that driving I did today." She checked her watch. "It's after nine o'clock. How are you doing?"

Nicole looked at me. "After this song, I'll be ready to go."

"I should get back and relieve Ingrid,' I said. "She's probably waiting up."

"I insist on driving you up the hill, Jillian," Ann said.

I smiled, grateful.

"If you insist."

A small light burned in the window. I found my key and unlocked the front door, tiptoeing inside, hoping not to wake Ingrid.

Teddy yipped at my arrival.

I gathered him in my arms and gave him a hug and a kiss before turning out the light.

"Let's be quiet," I whispered. "I think Ingrid's asleep."

I laid him on the bed, undressed, and slipped under the covers.

The bubble bath could wait until morning.

The girls' getaway was such a great idea. After the emotional roller coaster I'd been on with Vincent, I needed this.

Lord, please watch over Vincent. He's in some kind of trouble and isn't comfortable telling me what it is. Thank you for this getaway with my friends. Goodnight.

I turned over several times as I tried to get comfortable, finally managing to turn off my brain and go to sleep.

The sound of a dog barking woke me up.

I looked at the clock.

It was dawn.

CHAPTER FIVE

I heard sirens. Was there a fire?

Teddy whined and curled up next to me for comfort.

A text came in from Nicole:

You'd better come, police cars beneath our window.

I threw back the covers, put Teddy on the floor, and quickly dressed.

"We'd better go see what happened."

"Woof," he barked.

Ingrid was in the kitchen using her phone.

"What happened?" I asked.

"I'm not sure. I was texting Claire to make sure it wasn't her. She's not answering."

"Nicole told me the police were in the parking lot. We should go together."

"Okay, we'll take my car. It will be faster."

I grabbed a few snacks for Teddy and stuck them in my pocket just in case.

"Let's get your leash," I said.

Ingrid looked worried.

"Has anything like this ever happened before?" I asked.

"Not since I've been here."

When we drove in, police cars crowded the lot. An officer was putting crime scene tape around the dumpster area.

I looked up to see Ann and Nicole waving.

"Maybe they know something," Ingrid said. "Go on up and see what you can find out. I'll hold Teddy."

The door was ajar when I reached their suite.

"Come in," Nicole said.

Ann was standing at the window.

Nicole and I joined her and looked down at the dumpsters.

Two police officers went inside what I assumed was the kitchen entrance. They stayed a while.

"Last night we heard a commotion." Ann motioned to the scene below. "An argument of some sort."

"We almost called the front desk, but it ended." Nicole rubbed her hands. "I hope no one was hurt."

There was movement. Onlookers moved aside as a police van drove in.

Members of a medical team took a gurney from the back and wheeled it inside.

"This doesn't look good," I said. "I need to get Teddy. Ingrid has him down there."

"We're coming, too." Ann threw on a sweater and grabbed a passkey.

"Woof!" Teddy barked when he saw me. He wagged his tail happy to see me again.

I took him from Ingrid.

"I'm going to see what I can find out. Claire is okay. She's at home with Sam."

"Thank heavens!" I said.

I set Teddy on the ground and held his leash.

"Move aside please, coming through." The officer seemed to be the one in charge.

We moved aside as one of the medical team held the door while another wheeled out the gurney.

It was loaded with what appeared to be a body.

"Oh, dear!" I said to Ann and Nicole.

"Yeah, that's what I say," said a bystander.

The stocky spectator wore a plaid shirt and jeans, typical of the area residents, and had a receding hairline. He was tan, I assumed, from working outdoors.

"I found the back door locked this morning when I tried to make a produce delivery."

"What did you do?" Nicole asked.

"I went around and told the front desk. They led me to the kitchen. When I found it empty, I took a look around and asked them to check the walk-in freezer."

"Is that where you found the body?" I asked.

"Sorry." He rubbed his stomach. "I'm a little nauseated. Chef Gumm was way in the back lying face down. It looked like he'd been stabbed. He was ghost white being in the freezer so long. I guess he finally got what was coming to him."

Ann gasped at his words, but the man himself didn't seem too upset by what he'd said.

I stuck out my hand. "I'm Jillian Bradley. These are my friends, Ann Fieldman and Nicole King."

"Quincy Morgan. I work up the road over at Hunt's Produce Farm. I've never seen a body before."

We shook hands.

He shrugged. "Guess I'd better get going."

As he was leaving, another man, wearing a black, pillbox chef hat carrying an apron, came up to him.

"Hey, Quincy."

"Hey, Will. Ma'am, this is Will Pratt, Executive Sous Chef at the inn."

"Jillian Bradley. I'm sorry about Chef Gumm. What a terrible thing to happen. Will you take over for him?"

"At least until they hire somebody. I can handle things until they do. Hey, I'd better get going – Quincy, don't forget to stick the goods in the fridge."

"No problem. "As soon as the police finish with whatever they do, I'll see that it's done.

He turned to us. "I need to go, too, ladies. I need to get these boxes inside. Sorry if this ruined your stay."

"We'll talk to you later, Quincy."

You can be sure of that.

With all the distractions, I wasn't paying much attention to my small companion.

For some reason he yanked free and ran toward the gurney.

I tried to catch him but he escaped.

"Teddy, come back here, right this instant!"

The man who seemed to be in charge waved his arm.

"Someone get that dog out of the way."

Teddy ran straight toward him.

The man reached out and grabbed the runaway.

I made my way through the onlookers.

"I'm sorry, officer. Teddy fancies himself a sleuth dog and can't resist being part of an investigation."

With a cold stare, he handed him to me without a word.

"Bad dog!" I said.

Teddy cowered at the rebuke.

"Does your dog have police training?" The officer's voice held contempt.

I shook my head. "But he has found clues in murder investigations."

That roused the officer's attention.

"I'm busy right now, but if you have a card, I may want to talk to you later."

"My purse is at the cottage, but if you give me yours, I'll send my information."

"Fair enough. I'm Police Chief Mark Taylor, at your service, ma'am."

There was that "ma'am" again – a polite address to remind me I was a senior.

After taking the card, I introduced myself.

"I'm Jillian Bradley. I'm staying with Ingrid Sorenson just up the road."

I pointed to her cottage.

He nodded.

"So you're next door to Eva Gumm." He bowed his head. "We found her husband this morning."

"I heard. How tragic for her!"

An officer waved. "We're ready, sir."

Chief Taylor tipped his brow and joined his team.

After the chief left, Nicole and Ann caught up with Teddy and me.

"This sure puts a damper in our day." Ann put her hands on her hips. "What's your pleasure, Jillian? As if we couldn't guess."

"I know it's none of our business...."

"You're right about that," Nicole said.

"But I feel terrible for Chef Gumm's wife. We were getting acquainted yesterday. She seems like such a nice person for something awful like this to happen."

A text came in on my phone.

"It's Ingrid. She says she has to go to work and for us to make ourselves at home at her place."

"That might be a good idea." Nicole said. "I'll grab some pastries and coffees from Starbucks. There's one on Main Street we passed on our way in."

"And I'll go get our purses." Ann said.

"I'll wait here with Teddy. See you in a minute."

I took the card Chief Taylor gave me and sent him an email with my information.

The crowd dispersed after the police loaded the gurney and drove it away. Poor Chef Gumm.

I held Teddy close for comfort. "You wanted to meet that police chief, didn't you?"

"Woof!" he barked.

"Fritz is going to miss his master. I'm glad we're here. Eva may need us."

A little whine came from my small companion as if he understood what I was saying. Either that or he wanted to go play with Fritz.

Ann drove us to the cottage.

Next door, I noticed a police car parked in Eva's driveway.

I shook my head sadly. Maybe I could help console her – I hoped so.

We let ourselves in. The house was empty. Ingrid must have started her shift.

After hanging our wraps and purses on the coat rack, the three of us meandered into the kitchen.

"Today would be a good day to go shopping." Nicole set fresh fruit, muffins, and cups of orange juice on the table.

"It would be a good distraction." Ann found the coffee and made a pot. "What's the weather look like?"

I glanced out the window. "A few clouds. It might rain, but we have umbrellas.

"Look next door. Chief Taylor is coming out of Eva's house."

We watched as he put his arms around her and held her as she cried.

"How kind of him, don't you think?" I asked.

Ann lowered her chin and looked at Nicole.

"Kind?" Ann went to find coffee cups. "Is that what you think 'kind' looks like?"

"Let's not jump to conclusions." I selected a pretty mug and Ann poured my coffee. "He's probably a good friend. Remember, this is a small town."

"Then it shouldn't be that hard to find the murderer." Nicole took a bite of muffin and speared a strawberry with her fork.

We sat a moment drinking our coffee and eating our breakfast. After tossing Teddy a small bite, I studied the pumpkin muffin and wondered if Chef Gumm made it.

"Nicole, you said there was a commotion by the dumpsters last night."

"We both heard it." Ann refilled our coffee.

"First, a younger man stormed out the door," Nicole said. "Chef Gumm, at least I think it was him, it was dark, but there was a light, charged out after him yelling, and waving his fist."

"What happened next?" I asked.

"We heard them yell at each other." Nicole glanced at Ann. "We don't know what was said."

"But we did see Chef Gumm hit the younger man. Right in the jaw! After it happened, the chef went back inside and the young man left in his car."

"I see. I wonder if he came back later."

Nicole and Ann cleared the table and tidied the kitchen.

"The shops should be open," I said. "I'll get dressed and take Teddy for a walk. I'll meet you out front."

"Oh, there was one other thing." Nicole dried the last clean dish. "Someone drove out of the parking lot when all this happened. We heard the car."

"A witness?" I asked.

"It was a man." Nicole turned to Ann. "Did you recognize who it was?"

She thought a moment.

"It looked like the Head Sous Chef we met this morning, Will Pratt."

"If it wasn't him, I wonder who Chef Gumm was arguing with."

CHAPTER SIX

I looked for Eva and Fritz as we took our walk. An eerie silence surrounded her house. The blinds were closed – no way to tell if she was home.

Teddy kept pulling me toward Eva's, but I pulled him back.

"This will be a short walk, sweet doggie. We'll go down to the fishing dock and back."

He fell in line with my steps again. What a smart dog he was.

The lake was peaceful and still except for a lone canoer rowing far on the other side.

I glanced at the other dock to see if anyone was sitting in the Adirondack chairs.

They were empty.

Like me.

I so wanted Vincent and me to work. Being with him in Costa Rica as we explored waterfalls spilling into blue waters and watched a rare pair of scarlet macaws fly overhead were some of the happiest moments I'd known.

Stop daydreaming, Jillian.

Teddy was panting – I needed to get him some fresh water. If I didn't have my little companion, it would be so easy to fall into self-pity.

While he lapped, I went to my room and took his cheetah tote from the closet. He'd be easier to contain while we shopped.

My friends were waiting for us in front of the inn.

As we set off in the direction of Main Street, Ann glanced back.

"Things are sure quiet. Ingrid said the police were finished with forensics."

"I hope people don't start to leave like they did at the Ritz-Carlton in Half Moon Bay." Nicole turned to me. "Remember?"

"How could I forget? The guests here don't seem as uptight."

Main Street was a short walk taking only a few minutes. We looked into shops at a leisurely pace while Teddy napped in his tote.

Nicole found a cute mug as a souvenir.

Ann shopped for clothes.

I bought nothing. Besides having what I needed, I wasn't in the mood. I nodded to bouquets of fresh flowers.

"I'm going to get Eva this bouquet of daisies. She might appreciate the gesture."

"Good idea, Jillian," Nicole said. "We'll meet you up at the register."

"By the way, is anyone else hungry?" I asked. "It's almost noon."

Teddy woke up and stretched. Did he recognize the word "hungry?"

"I'd like to try The Cottage." Ann selected a red sweater coat and paid the shopkeeper.

"Anywhere is fine with me," I said.

"I saw they have flat bread pizzas on the menu when I ordered our breakfasts." Nicole looked expectant. "Plus they may not mind us eating outside on the patio with Teddy."

We headed for food.

Teddy was no problem, thankfully.

A server seated us and took our orders.

I read his name badge. Sam Hunt. He did seem familiar. I waited until he brought our drinks.

"Excuse me," I said. "Are you Claire's husband?"

His eyes narrowed. "Yeah, why?"

"I'm Jillian Bradley – these are my friends, Ann Fieldman and Nicole King. We're from Clover Hills."

A smile broke out on his face.

"Really? No kidding? I used to live there."

"I know, Sam. I was at your wedding."

He looked sheepish.

"Wait, Claire did mention you were coming. I didn't know you were here."

"Terrible business this morning about Chef Gumm." Nicole sipped her water.

"Ah, yeah...terrible. No great loss, though."

Ann bored into his eyes.

"What makes you say that?"

He shrugged. "Gumm was a pain. I couldn't stand him."

We looked at each other with raised eyebrows.

"You're the second person this morning who made a remark like that." I gave Teddy a pat.

"What's in the tote?" Sam asked.

Teddy poked his head up.

"Aw, you have a Yorkie." Sam smiled. "Claire's been asking for one, but we can't afford it yet."

He excused himself and went inside to wait on other customers since The Cottage was getting busy.

"Interesting." Nicole seemed thoughtful.

"What is?" Ann asked.

Nicole turned to her. "Ann, don't you think Sam looks like the guy arguing with Chef Gumm?"

"Oh my, you're right! When he comes with our orders, let's check out his face."

"I did. This isn't good, ladies," I said. "There's a small bruise on his cheek. It could implicate him in the murder."

I silently prayed Sam wasn't the killer, for Claire's sake.

"This is bad. If Ann and I tell the police what we saw and heard in the parking lot last night, it will definitely make Sam a suspect."

"And if we don't tell, we're withholding evidence."

"Exactly. Ladies, we have our work cut out."

"Jillian," Nicole said. "You have that look."

"Woof!" Teddy barked.

I reached over and kissed his head.

"I think Teddy knew we would be needed. That's why he ran to Chief Taylor."

Sam returned with our meals.

"Ladies." He set our food on the table. "Can I bring you anything else?"

We didn't say a word. The small bruise on his cheek made us tongue-tied.

I shook my head.

"We're fine for now, thanks."

"After our jaunt into town and the amount of food I ate, I'm going to need a nap." Nicole yawned and covered her mouth.

"Let's meet up for tea in the lobby. Ingrid may watch Teddy for me since her shift ends about that time. I'll see you later."

Ann and Nicole disappeared into the inn.

I attached Teddy's leash and set him on the ground so I wouldn't have to carry him up the hill."

"We should be ready for a nap by the time we get home, too, little fella."

Teddy yipped.

Eva still wasn't at home from the looks of her empty driveway. The blinds were still closed.

A pang of sympathy for her pierced my heart.

"Let's get your leash off, boy." I unhooked it from his collar and hung it on a coat rack by the front door.

Teddy marched into the kitchen for some water.

The iron bed looked inviting.

I opened the window for some fresh air and took off my shoes.

Teddy came in and looked up at me as if to say, "You can put me on the bed – I'm ready for our nap."

I was grateful for the way he made me smile.

We lay down and took a short nap. I found a pretty quilt in the closet to use for a cover.

The sound of a car door slamming woke me up. Was Ingrid back from work?

Teddy poked his head up, alert for action.

I slipped on my shoes, smoothed down my hair, and picked him up to go check things out.

The clock told me Ingrid wasn't due home yet. I looked out the front window to see if Eva was home.

Her car was parked in the driveway.

I wondered if it was too soon to pay her a visit. When I thought about it, though, I remembered how much I appreciated people's support when my first husband died in Vietnam.

"Let's go see Eva and Fritz, Teddy."

"Woof!" he barked. The way his bark almost sounded muffled always caused me to smile. How I loved him.

Fritz barked behind the door when I knocked.

It took a minute for to Eva answer after she peered through the blinds to see who it was.

I didn't mind.

She opened the door slightly and looked at me with swollen eyes.

"Jillian, come in."

"I'm so sorry, Eva. I brought you some flowers."

As if in a daze, she reached out and took them.

"That's very kind of you. Would you like to come in? I could use some company."

"Sure."

Fritz wagged his tail when he saw Teddy.

"I'm glad you brought him. It will help Fritz take his mind off...."

She broke down.

I removed the leash and the dogs raced upstairs.

I put my arms around her. "I know it hurts. Cry all you want. It helps, trust me."

I glanced upstairs concerned about the dogs being where we couldn't see them.

"They'll be fine. Sorry for my outburst. Please have a seat. I'll make us some coffee. It seems to help."

"That sounds good."

While Eva made coffee, I glanced around the room.

The furnishings were elegant but didn't seem to fit the rather plain house. It made me wonder about her background.

"Here you go." Eva handed me a mug. "Black, right?"

I smiled. "Thanks."

"I noticed your wedding photo on the mantle. Your husband was a handsome young man."

She took a sip and stared at the floor.

"I identified Gumby's body."

"That must have been difficult. Is that what you called him?"

She raised her eyes and nodded.

"I was the only one he allowed to call him that. Sometimes I heard others call him Gumby but only behind his back."

"Eva, do you have any idea who would want to kill him? "

Teddy scampered downstairs closely followed by Fritz.

"Is it okay if they go outside in the dog run? It's fenced," she asked.

"For a little while. I need to keep a close watch on Teddy. He's small."

Eva led the dogs outside and locked them in the run.

"Now we can talk in peace."

She settled on the sofa and picked up her mug.

I leaned back to listen.

"Gumby was catering a party for Mother when I met him. I was smitten with his Salzburger Nockerl."

I gave a quizzical look.

"Before you ask, it's a sweet soufflé served as a dessert in Salzburg. Gumby said later it reminded him of my chest, to put it politely, because the row of soufflés looks like yellow mountains...."

"And the reference goes along with the word Nockerl. I get it."

Eva looked up at nothing.

"He was so charming when I first met him. A completely different man than he was in the last few years."

"What changed?"

She took a drink of coffee before answering.

"The life of an executive chef is grueling. Even with great help, a chef has to keep up the creation of new menus and recipes as the seasons change."

"That can be stressful unless one enjoys the creativity. When he served us the other evening, he seemed happy with what he was doing."

"I'm glad to hear that. He did love the creative part but hated to deal with vendors and accounting."

"I never thought about it. Most of us probably think a head chef wears a smock, dons a tall white hat, and creates dishes as works of art."

"His specialty was pastries. I finally learned to throw away at least half of every pastry he brought me to keep from gaining weight. Secretly of course."

"I do the same thing."

I finished my coffee and set the mug on a coaster.

"Regarding your question, Jillian, I've asked myself the same one over and over again, but it makes no sense. Gumby could be irritating, but not to the point where someone would kill him."

I thought about the incident near the dumpsters but said nothing.

"Who would he have been with late at night like that? You said sometimes he worked until 2 a.m."

"Some of the kitchen staff, I suppose. There may have been someone else working at the inn. I don't know, Jillian. The whole thing seems impossible!"

"So you know them pretty well."

"Yes, except for some of the housekeepers, but Gumby wouldn't have contact with them. Unless...."

"Unless what?"

"Oh, nothing. I was thinking about servers taking room service up from the kitchen. I suppose Mark could check who was on duty last night."

"Mark? You mean Chief Taylor?"

She blushed.

"Yes. We've been friends forever. Everyone in Lake Placid knows everyone else. It's a small town.

"My parents ran the inn until Dad died and Mother's health began to fail. Drew took over when she started getting confused. The hotel's been in my family since it was built in 1924."

A flickering in her eyes told me Eva was hiding something.

"Chief Taylor seems nice. Did you know him growing up?"

She stood and paced as if I made her nervous talking about Mark Taylor.

"We went to high school together. Mother insisted I go to a private one, but it was painfully small. I only lasted a year. After that, she allowed me to attend Lake Placid High."

Her mother sounded controlling.

"I assume there weren't many students. This is a small town, as you said."

"Very few. Can I get you more coffee?"

"Yes, thanks."

Eva seemed nervous. I needed to leave.

"On second thought, Eva, I'll take a rain check on the coffee. I'm sure you need to rest."

"I'll get Teddy for you."

The dogs raced back inside.

I put Teddy's leash on him and led him to the door.

"I appreciate the flowers, Jillian. We'll talk more tomorrow. I'm overwhelmed with things to do. Drew is coming in a few minutes to help me sort things out."

"I understand about the details. Thanks for the coffee. I'll see you tomorrow. Get some rest."

She nodded as Teddy and I stepped outside, and slowly closed the door.

I recalled the loneliness of being recently widowed – the quiet house, friends who stayed away because they didn't know what to say, the way my life changed.

But Eva had her brother who was probably lonely, too.

CHAPTER SEVEN

Ingrid walked in the door and hung her purse on the coat rack. "Am I glad that shift is over!"

Teddy lay curled in my lap, exhausted from his romp with Fritz. I gently moved him to a pillow at the end of the sofa to make room.

"Why don't I make us a cup of tea? You can put your feet up and tell me what's happening in the investigation. I can find my way around the kitchen."

"Thanks."

She smiled, sat down on the sofa, and kicked off her shoes.

I returned with the tea service – two china cups, milk, sugar, and a lovely pot of Earl Grey. I set the tray on the tufted ottoman, and turned to Ingrid.

"Milk? Sugars?" I asked.

"Just a little milk and no sugar, thanks."

I stirred a large spoonful of sugar into my tea, and turned to her to listen."

"The police aren't saying, hush-hush you know, but from what I've heard from some of the staff, it wasn't a robbery."

"Does everyone have alibis? There I go, thinking like a detective."

"Yes, but you have experience, Jillian. Chief Taylor is still talking to people. How can even *our* alibis hold up? We were in separate rooms when he was murdered."

"You have a valid point. Ingrid, I need your opinion."

"Ask away."

"Would you withhold evidence to protect a friend or loved one?"

"Depends on whether or not I believed they were guilty."

"That's what I think."

She looked at me sideways.

"Who are you trying to protect?"

"Sam."

"My son-in-law Sam? Why do you think he needs protecting?"

I sighed. "I might as well tell you. The night Chef Gumm was murdered my friends witnessed an argument near the dumpsters."

"And they think it was Sam?"

"We're almost positive it was. They saw Chef Gumm strike a young man who looked very much like Sam. When we were at The Cottage having lunch today, Sam was our server."

"Did he say he argued with Gumm?"

"He didn't have to. There was a mark on his cheek in the exact spot where Gumm struck the person."

Ingrid looked serious.

"Now I must tell *you* something in confidence."

I leaned in. "I must ask you to let me share whatever it is with Ann and Nicole if I think it will help Sam."

"Agreed. Claire was constantly fighting off Gumm's unwanted advances. Sam was livid! A few days ago he told her he was going to have it out."

"He may have."

My heart sank.

Ingrid bowed her head a moment.

"Jillian, would you pray for Sam right now? I think he's going to need it."

I left Teddy with Ingrid while I dined with my friends at the inn. She insisted on feeding him supper and seemed to enjoy his company.

The inn was buzzing with people. A line had already formed for *The View* restaurant when we arrived.

"Jillian!" Ann waved standing at the reservation desk. Nicole was with her. Claire motioned for me to join them.

"Our turn?" I said.

"Right this way, ladies." Claire led us to a table overlooking the lake and handed us menus. "Enjoy."

After she left, I turned toward my friends.

"She doesn't seem upset, does she?"

Ann observed. "She looks happy, if you ask me."

"I agree." Nicole set her menu down. "More relieved, I'd say, than happy."

We made our selections and gave our orders to the server. He returned with a basket of homemade rolls and a plate of butter curls.

I selected a hard roll and spread it with butter.

"I talked to Ingrid about Sam. My intuition tells me we should find out as much as possible about what happened the night of the murder before we go to the police."

"I agree," Ann said. "You know they'd arrest him if they thought he'd fought with Gumm."

"It would ruin his reputation, too." Nicole selected a rye roll, broke it in half, and took a bite.

"At least I found out the reason Sam hated Gumm. Ingrid said Claire was being sexually harassed."

"Sounds like a motive for premeditated murder to me," Ann said.

"Or not," I said. "We need to look closer at who could have hated him enough to kill him."

"Of course, it could have been something else." Nicole chewed thoughtfully.

The server brought our salads and refilled our water.

"Let's hear it, Nicole." I sprinkled my salad with salt and pepper.

"I can't believe you eat salad with no dressing," Ann said.

"It's a way to save on calories. I like the way the veggies taste without it, besides, the salt and pepper mixed with the juices from the veggies creates its own dressing."

Nicole set her fork down. "What if there's something going on we can't see. Sometimes we learn the victims get killed because they know something, or they're in the wrong place at the wrong time."

"She's right, Jillian."

"If there is another motive, we'll have to find it." I lifted my glass to my friends.

They raised theirs, too.

"To success!"

We clinked our glasses together.

"To success," they said.

The entrées arrived.

"The trout looks delicious," Ann said, as the server presented my plate.

"Our family used to trout fish whenever we went camping. Dad would cook them over an open fire."

"Sounds like wonderful memories," Nicole said.

"Most of them were except for the time my dad rested his hand against a hot stove pipe. It hurt so badly! I can still remember him yelling an obscenity and my mother scolding him."

"I saw a number of fishermen along the riverbanks when we first drove in." Ann inhaled the aroma of her grilled lamb loin as it arrived.

"Your dinner will be up soon," the server said to Nicole.

"Please go ahead, ladies," she said. "Enjoy them while they're hot."

We waited for 10 minutes until her entrée finally arrived.

"I'm so sorry, ma'am," the server said. "The chef says there will be no charge for your meal."

"How kind. Thank you." Nicole tasted her herb stuffed quail and nodded approval.

"I would imagine there might be tension in the kitchen with someone new in charge." I took the last bite of trout.

"And yet, look around – the restaurant is packed," Ann said.

I glanced around and quickly looked back. "Don't stare, but I see the same man who flirted with me the other night sitting at a table with some woman."

"I wonder if she's his wife," Nicole said.

As we finished, the server deftly removed our plates.

"You may take mine, too," Nicole said to him. "I'd like to save room for dessert."

"Would anyone be interested in sharing an Apple Tart?" I asked.

"Sounds perfect," Ann said.

Nicole nodded.

As we ate our dessert and sipped cappuccinos, the man who flirted with me the night before left with the woman he was sitting with. It caused me to wonder.

"Ladies," I said. "If we're going to help steer the police away from Sam, we'd better reconstruct the events on the night Gumm was murdered."

"I agree." Ann laid her napkin on the table signaling she'd finished.

"Let's move upstairs where we can talk in private." Nicole said.

"Okay, but I must watch the time – Ingrid will probably want to go to bed soon and I need to rescue her from Teddy," I said.

After we were inside their room, Nicole went to the desk, took out the leather information folder, and removed two pieces of stationary.

"This should do," she said. "I'll be secretary."

We sat huddled together on the sofa and tried to recollect the facts.

"We know Sam and Gumm argued on the night of the murder – that's one fact." Nicole entered the note.

"We think we saw the sous chef, Will Pratt, drive out of the parking lot during the fight," Ann said.

Nicole kept writing.

"Ingrid said Gumm made unwanted advances toward Claire. That may have been why Sam wanted to confront him." Nicole looked up.

"Jillian, didn't you say Gumm's wife...."

"Eva?"

"Yes, you thought there might be something between her and Chief Taylor."

"No, it was Ann who thought that, remember?"

I reflected.

"Now that you mention it, when I talked to Eva this afternoon, she seemed uncomfortable when I brought him up."

"Got it." Nicole continued to write. "What else do we know?"

We sat and thought a minute.

"A man flirted with Jillian at dinner." Ann smiled.

"That probably isn't important." I blushed.

"Unless it puts him at the scene of the crime." Nicole made a note.

"And don't forget we saw the same guy tonight at dinner. It could be important." Ann looked at me.

I shrugged.

"Let's not forget what happened this morning. When we were standing in the crowd, I talked to a man who mentioned Gumm got what was coming to him."

Nicole looked up. "What was his name, do you remember?"

"No. But I remember where he worked. Hunt's Produce Farm."

Ann furrowed her brow.

"I wonder if it's related to Sam Hunt."

"Only one way to find out. I think I'll pay them a visit."

I cast my mind back to the parking lot.

"Will Pratt might also throw some light onto what happened around that time since he left late."

"Good point, Jillian," Ann said.

I smiled.

"I think I may have another."

Nicole paused.

"And that would be?"

"We should probably talk to the young man working the desk that evening– his name was John, remember, Ann?"

"I do. You made a comment about his name badge. You're right – he could have seen something. That desk is pretty centralized."

Nicole leaned back and studied the list.

"That makes at least six or seven places to start."

Ann stood and walked to the window.

"Let me work on Will Pratt. Jillian, see if you can get his schedule from Ingrid so I can 'bump into him' when he gets off work."

Nicole stuck the list back inside the black folder.

"And why don't I pay a visit to Hunt's Produce Farm? I might learn something about the person who delivers to the inn."

I gathered my purse and headed for the door.

"I'll keep talking to Ingrid and see if I can learn anymore about Eva and Chief Taylor. Ingrid may also be able to arrange for me to talk to John, the desk clerk.

"Ladies, it's time we went to work."

The walk back to Ingrid's was refreshing in the cool night air. The exercise felt good after a rich dessert.

Eva's house was dark except for a single light upstairs.

I refrained from knocking to allow her some privacy.

Ingrid was in the living room when I came in.

Teddy yipped and wagged his tail until I thought it would come off. He was so happy to see me.

I scooped him up and gave him a hug and a kiss.

"I hope he wasn't too much trouble."

Ingrid stretched.

"No trouble at all, but he may want to go outside."

"I'll take him for a walk while you get ready for bed."

At the word "walk," Teddy wriggled from my arms to the floor and stood alert at the coat rack."

"He wants me to attach his leash. This dog is always one-step ahead of me. Thanks for watching him."

"No problem." She smiled at him, and went to her room.

"Come on, boy. Let's take a walk down by the lake."

Teddy and I headed toward the fishing dock, a popular rendezvous spot it seemed.

A couple who'd been sitting in the Adirondack chairs stood to leave as two men approached.

I recognized one of the men was Drew Olson, the inn's general manager.

The other man was the same man who flirted with me the night before and we'd seen at dinner this evening.

What was he doing with Eva's brother?

I tiptoed away back to the cottage, unseen.

CHAPTER EIGHT

Teddy and I slipped in quietly. I took off his leash and hung it on the coat rack while he marched into the kitchen for a drink of water and I readied for bed.

Even after a nice hot bubble bath, I wasn't sleepy. I donned my robe and slippers and went to the kitchen for a glass of water.

Teddy was right at my heels as if making sure I wasn't going to leave him again.

"I know, boy, but sometimes I have to leave you. Ingrid's son-in-law needs our help."

He cocked his head when I mentioned Ingrid.

"Woof!" he barked softly.

It was as if he knew Ingrid was asleep and he needed to use his "inside" voice like mothers tell their children.

"I love you, sweet doggie."

After placing him next to me on the sofa, I picked up a travel magazine and thumbed the pages. I returned to the cover and noted the date. 1980.

A closer look at the table of contents revealed an article on Drew Olson, winner of the bronze medal in freestyle skiing.

I read all about the man until I couldn't keep my eyes open. This must be some family, I thought.

Teddy was asleep.

I gathered his soft tiny body, carried him to the bed, and put him on his towel.

"Night-night, little one."

A spritz of perfume gave a pleasant send-off to sleep.

Goodnight, Lord.

Tomorrow, I would look for a way to talk to the desk clerk.

I woke to the sound of Teddy scratching on the door. Did I oversleep? It was only 7:20 a.m.

I caught a whiff of bacon.

"So that's why you're awake."

He cocked his head and looked so innocent as if to say, "It's not just the bacon, I need to go outside."

I threw on my robe and hopped into my slippers ready to take him out.

"Good morning, Jillian." Ingrid was dressed, ready for the day.

"Morning. I'll be right back. Teddy needs outside for a minute."

"I'm making homemade waffles and bacon."

"They smell wonderful."

Since I wasn't fully dressed, I took Teddy out back.

He sniffed around, and found a spot.

The beauty of Mirror Lake stopped me. The reflection of fall foliage against the majestic Adirondacks with fog rolling in was magnificent.

A slight breeze ruffled my hair.

Church bells rang in the distance.

I took time to pray.

Ingrid served breakfast in her bright cozy kitchen. The waffles were crispy and delicious.

Teddy stood at attention by my feet.

"Don't worry, sweet dog. I'll make your breakfast after I've eaten mine."

I gave him a tiny bite of my bacon.

"Do you like the maple syrup?" she asked.

I hesitated.

She smiled.

"Me, too. I can't tell the difference between real and imitation."

I couldn't resist.

"What about relationships? Can you tell the difference between say for instance a happy marriage verses a supposedly happy marriage?"

Ingrid sipped her coffee.

"It would depend on how well you knew the couple. I know Claire and Sam are happy for instance because I'm close to Claire as her mother."

"What about a neighbor?"

"A neighbor might be more difficult to determine unless there was camaraderie between said neighbors."

I waited to hear what she would surmise.

"Now, if you're referring to one of my neighbors in particular, I could say, from what I'd heard from others and also coming from said neighbor's house, no, theirs not a happy marriage."

I nodded.

"Would you say jealousy may have caused the unhappiness?"

Ingrid considered.

"A strong possibility and could have come from both husband and wife."

"I see. It sounds complex."

"Refill?"

"Thank you, I'd love some."

Ingrid drained the rest of the coffee into my mug.

"So, hypothetically, do you think jealousy would be a strong enough motive to kill in their case?" I asked.

"I do. It's rumored the husband abused the wife. Whether or not he did so because of jealousy I don't know."

"Wives have been known to kill abusive husbands."

"And husbands have been known to abuse unfaithful wives."

It was a good point.

Chef Gumm displayed a temper or he wouldn't have hit Sam. He may have hit Eva, too. If he did, perhaps Chief Taylor knew about it. It was a small town.

"I'm sorry to be so morbid, but I am curious."

I served Teddy his breakfast of cooked chicken, whole wheat bread, and part of a fruit cup.

He refused to eat at first and gave me a look.

"I'm sorry. I forgot the cheese, didn't I?"

Problem solved.

"Why don't we take a look at your garden before your shift?"

"I'd be delighted. I'll wash up while you get ready."

A denim shirt, layered with a tan cashmere sweater and pearls, plus a comfortable pair of my favorite jeans and voila! I was dressed.

I ran a comb through my hair, did my makeup, and spritzed perfume on my neck and wrists.

Teddy watched my every move and followed me outside after I slipped on his leash.

Ingrid's garden was a magnificent array of color. Pink New Zealand asters, toad lilies with intricate, orchid-like flowers, and cheery yellow flowers of goldenrod mingled with Russian sage with airy blue flowers and silvery foliage.

"Umm." I took in the scent. "The sage has such a lovely smell."

Teddy sniffed the air as if to mimic me.

"Gardening in zone 4 is quite different than in the Bay Area." Ingrid snipped some Japanese anemone for the cottage. "Here the winter starts about now in mid-September."

"We don't really have a winter, do we?"

"Not compared to Lake Placid. The snowfall is incredible!"

"Perfect for the winter Olympics. Speaking of, I noticed a magazine last night that had an article on Drew Olson. He won a bronze in 1980."

"I'd forgotten I still had it. He gave me a copy when I moved in. He said it had some gardening articles but I figured he wanted to let me know he was a 'somebody.'"

"Some people are like that. I must ask you about one of the staff. His name is John and he was working as the desk clerk the night Chef Gumm was murdered."

"John Peterson. He lives in the same apartments as Claire and Sam. Why are you interested in him?"

I shrugged.

"We think he may have seen something the night of the murder."

The "we" was not lost on Ingrid.

"We? As in you, Nicole, and Ann?"

I could only smile.

"Good."

She removed her gloves and walked to sit on the porch.

"I had a hard time sleeping last night worrying about Sam. Claire said Chief Taylor wanted to talk to him whenever it was convenient."

"Oh, dear. My friends and I had better work fast."

"John Peterson works mid-shift today. I saw the schedule. The best time to catch him would be right after work at The Cottage.

"Is that the local hangout?

"It is for the staff."

"Perfect. Thanks. Oh by the way, what's the schedule for Will Pratt?"

"He takes a break about three. I often pass him when I'm heading home."

"Thanks, Ingrid. You've been a big help."

"Anything for Claire. She's my only child."

"I know."

"Would you like a ride to the inn?"

"I'll walk – It's such a beautiful morning and I need the exercise. Thanks anyway. Have a good shift."

Ingrid settled into her car and drove away.

I took out my phone and called Ann.

"What's on the agenda today?" I asked.

"Besides doing our little snooping?"

"This is a getaway, Ann."

"I was only teasing. Nicole suggested a drive over to Saratoga Springs and Lake George. She talked to a guest at breakfast who raved over the color."

"A leaf peeper, huh?"

Ann chuckled.

"We can also stop in at Hunt's Produce Farm. I believe it isn't too far."

"Nicole is nodding her head. We're ready whenever you are."

"Teddy and I are leaving right now. We'll see you in a few minutes."

As I approached the parking lot behind the inn, I noticed Drew Olson getting out of his car.

He smiled when he saw Teddy and me and waved.

"Good morning, Jillian."

I waved back and took out my phone to text Ann to tell her I'd arrived.

Drew headed straight for me.

"It's a splendid day, isn't it? I like the pearls."

I blushed. "Thank you."

He reached down to pet Teddy. "Where are you two off to this morning?"

"We thought a drive to Saratoga Springs and Lake George would be nice."

I waited for Ann and Nicole to come through the back door.

"It's the perfect time of year – the leaves are at their height of color."

He straightened up and stepped closer.

"If you'd like, I could take you on the ski jump to see a real view. Promise me you'll take me up on my offer."

How I would have loved to be able to fib right now about being afraid of heights, but my conscience wouldn't allow it.

"Thank you for the invitation. I'll tell my friends."

How was that for a side step?

He looked a bit disappointed.

"Certainly. I'm free tomorrow morning. Shall we say 10 o'clock?"

"Let me check and I'll let you know. I'll need to find a sitter for Teddy. I'd hate for something to happen to him."

He reached for his phone. "Give me your email and I'll add it to my contacts. I'll ask Eva if she wouldn't mind watching Teddy for you."

Smooth.

I turned to find Nicole and Ann walking toward us.

"Good." He smiled at them. "Why don't we invite them now?"

After the acceptance of Drew's invitation, my friends and I climbed in the SUV. No one said anything at first.

Nicole broke the awkward silence.

"What was that all about, Jillian?"

"He was being polite. Perhaps he's lonely and saw a chance to be with three fascinating women."

"Two of which are married, I might add." Ann started the car, backed out, and drove down the hill to take a right on Main Street.

"Let's just enjoy the drive," I said.

"Woof!" Teddy barked.

"He probably can't wait to sniff the ground at our first rest stop."

As we passed The Cottage directly across the street from the inn, I was reminded of the desk clerk, John.

"Ladies, Ingrid told me the desk clerk I want to talk to gets off around four this afternoon. She says he usually hangs out afterward at The Cottage."

"I'm sure we'll be back in plenty of time." Ann drove slowly through the main part of town.

"She also said Will Pratt takes a break mid-afternoon."

"Good," Nicole said. "Ann, you can try and talk to him."

"And there's something else – bad news I'm afraid, although it's a mystery," I said.

"What?" Ann asked.

"Ingrid said the police want to talk to Sam."

Nicole turned to me.

"At least we didn't have to report what we saw in the parking lot. It looks like someone else did."

"I'm glad we didn't have to," Ann said. "Someone might have observed Claire's harassment by Chef Gumm and mentioned it to the police. It would be like waving a red flag at Sam."

The drive was lovely along state roads through the Adirondack Mountains. The fog, however, seem to never let go.

"You're suddenly quiet, Jillian. Ann looked in the rear view mirror. "Vincent?"

"Not this time. There isn't much I can do about that man since he won't even talk to me."

"Care to tell us what's bothering you?" Nicole asked.

Teddy stretched trying to get comfortable in his dog seat.

I scratched behind his ears.

"You're being a very good boy, Teddy."

I shook my head.

"Ingrid and I had a hypothetical conversation this morning about Eva and her marriage. There were overtones of possible abuse from her husband."

Nicole turned in the front seat and looked at me.

"Really? That's interesting. You don't think she killed him, do you?"

"No. Even if she was abused, Eva talks as if their relationship was normal. Of course we don't really know, do we?"

Ann came to a stop sign and nodded to the left of the road.

"There's a nice looking rest stop if you'd like to get out and stretch your legs."

Teddy yipped as if he understood perfectly what Ann said. The dog was psychic!

"Teddy would appreciate a break." I unbuckled his seat as Ann pulled over.

The view was nothing but a dense forest situated along the rippling river.

Nicole mused.

"This empty terrain is such a contrast to the busy traffic of the Bay Area. I find it refreshing."

"I'm glad we came, too," Ann said. "Except for the murder."

"It was destiny, ladies." I held Teddy's leash while he explored along the riverbank.

He started to jerk away but I held him fast.

"What is it, boy?"

"Woof, woof!" he barked.

Up ahead a squatting figure dressed in camouflage turned toward us. He held a fishing pole and reeled in the line.

"Teddy, be quiet! You'll scare away the fish." I patted his nose to make my point.

The man waved as if he knew us.

It was Chief Taylor.

CHAPTER NINE

The chief reached out to the end of his line and caught hold of a wiggling fish. A huge smile crossed his face as he unhooked his catch and stuffed it into the woven basket he carried.

Teddy wagged his tail and cocked his head as the chief approached.

"Hello ladies, Teddy. Out for some leaf peeping I see."

"I'm surprised to see you out here..." I said.

He wiped a few beads of perspiration from his brow.

"It is Saturday. Even we poor civil servants need to relax on the weekends."

Ann and Nicole found a flat rock to sit on under a shade tree.

A hat would have come in handy to protect my fair skin against the bright sunlight – I wished I had brought one. Instead, I stepped into the shade next to the rock for some protection.

Teddy sniffed the chief – did he detect the fish?

"How's the investigation coming?" Ann asked.

"We're working on it. I can tell you we have a person of interest."

"Sam Hunt?" Nicole asked.

A look of astonishment crossed his face.

"You ladies need to let me do my job. I don't want your help, do you understand? I don't care what you've done in other investigations."

I stood my ground.

"Chief, Ingrid Sorenson is a friend of ours. Friends help each other, do *you understand?*" I said.

"Okay, I understand where you're coming from. I'm only trying to keep you ladies safe. The less you know about the investigation the better."

"I think we know how things work, Chief." I picked up Teddy. "We probably shouldn't take up anymore of your leisure time."

He stood silent as we got back inside the SUV and drove away.

"You were pretty hard on him back there," Nicole said.

"I know. Not everyone is as driven as I am. But the fact is he never even had the courtesy to acknowledge an email I sent."

"He made himself quite clear just now. I'll say one thing for you, though – you're never boring!" Ann said.

We chuckled as we resumed the scenic drive through breathtaking fall color.

Not too far up the road a small billboard loomed – *Hunt's Produce Farm* ahead two miles.

"I see it, Jillian. Ann – let's take the next exit."

"I hope they have food. I'm hungry!"

My friends smiled at me.

Ann made the turn onto a dirt road and followed it about a mile until we reached the farm complex.

A large building housed the retail store in front with long rows of covered greenhouses in back.

I put Teddy in his tote before we went in.

"Be a good dog and don't bark!" I said.

He obediently settled down and closed his eyes.

Inside the store were rows and rows of fresh produce. Boxes were filled with a variety of apples – Gala, Golden Delicious, Fuji, and my favorite to make apple pies – McIntosh. Jars of yummy blackberry jam, jellies, and other sundry items lined the shelves.

I searched until I found what I was looking for – a refrigerator full of gourmet sandwiches and healthy looking salads.

The tuna and sprouts Salad Nicoise had my name on it. Perfect for lunch.

"I found food." I waved at my friends, took the salad from the fridge, and carried it to the counter.

Teddy popped his head up when I mentioned food.

I took out a small treat and gave it to him.

Ann chose a sandwich and Nicole selected a chef salad.

"We have drinks, too, if you like." The cashier nodded to a refrigerator next to the counter.

"This is an amazing farm," I said. "I write a national gardening column – I'm Jillian Bradley."

"Nan Pritchard. I think I've heard of your column –Mr. Hunt, the owner, has mentioned it."

Ann and Nicole stepped up to pay.

These are my friends from home."

Nan nodded.

"Would it be possible to look around?" I selected a bottle of pink lemonade and paid for my purchases.

"Sure. I'll text the manager to let him know you're coming in a few minutes."

"Thanks. We'll want to eat our lunch first. Oh, is it okay to take my dog along? I promise he'll be good."

Nan smiled. "We love dogs. I'm sure he won't be any trouble."

She motioned to the right. "There are tables and chairs around the corner."

As we ate, a few customers strolled around the store. I broke off a tiny piece of egg from my salad and fed it to Teddy.

"Shall we?" I asked after wiping my lips and reapplying lipstick.

Inside the first greenhouse, several men worked cultivating seeds, examining seedlings, and re-potting larger specimens.

"Hello, ladies." A man in overalls introduced himself and offered to show us around.

"We're staying at the Mirror Lake Inn." I took a pinch of soil and gave it a sniff. "Chef Gumm mentioned your produce on the last night he worked there."

The worker shook his head.

"That was bad business. One of our workers told us about finding him in the freezer. Hey, he's coming in right now."

Our guide waved to the man we met in the parking lot on the morning the body was found. It was Quincy Morgan – the man we came to see.

"I have to check on some seed tests but he can show you around."

Quincy gave a look of recognition, or was it trepidation?

"Show these ladies around the complex, okay? Thanks, Quincy."

"Didn't we meet the other morning?" I asked.

"Yeah. I recognize your dog."

He gave Teddy a pat.

"What brings you ladies way out here?"

Ann picked up an arugula seedling nestled in a black plastic pot. "Jillian's a gardening columnist and can't resist anything to do with plants."

He shrugged.

"I'll show you around."

Quincy led us from greenhouse number one to the next one.

"The plants are given a chance to mature in here before we plant them outside."

Row upon row of lettuce varieties and herbs of every kind grew in flats.

"Who do you supply besides the public?" Nicole asked.

"Mirror Lake Inn is our main client but there're some changes going on which could change that."

"I'd be interested to hear about it. I'm into economics, you might say."

Good one, Nicole.

"Most of the large hotels do business with an exchange which recently formed. It lets suppliers charge a fair price for goods."

"What about this farm?" Ann asked.

"The owner is still trying to decide. I don't know what's going to happen now that Chef Gumm is gone. And good riddance, I say."

"You didn't like him I take it." I lifted a pot of lemongrass to smell.

"No. I thought he was rude and a snob. He always talked down to me. Right now Hunt's is the sole supplier for Mirror Lake. Mr. Hunt had a special price arrangement to get exclusivity or some word like that."

"Exclusivity?" I asked.

"Yeah. That's the word he used. I bet now we can supply other places and get a better price. Heck, I might even get a raise after all these years."

Quincy led us to the last greenhouse in the row.

"Here's where we keep our soil and supplies."

I noticed a room in back separated from the rest of the operation.

"What's in there?" I asked.

Quincy smiled.

"It's home for some of us. Me, for one."

He looked a little embarrassed at the fact.

"I'd say you had a great commute," Ann said.

He nodded.

"I suppose. Well, that's about it except for showing you the fields, which are fallow now. The frost is due any day. Is there anything else I can help you with?"

He led us outside where storm clouds were gathering.

"Out of curiosity, how long have you worked here?" Nicole asked.

"Ever since Sam left for school – he's the owner's son. You might say I took his place.

There was a touch of irony in his voice.

"It's been an interesting tour, thank you," Nicole said.

"We'd better be getting back on the road." Ann started to walk toward the car.

"Thanks, Quincy. I hope things work out for you." I took Teddy from his tote, attached his leash, and let him sniff the ground before getting back into the SUV.

He stood watching us until we drove out of sight.

"Well that was interesting," Ann said as she turned onto the main road. "What do you think, Jillian?"

"Did anyone else besides me get the feeling Quincy wasn't all that happy about his living situation?"

"I did notice all the other workers were much younger. He may resent other farms in the exchange getting paid more," Nicole said. "That's the impression he gave me, anyway."

"Sam might know more about it. We should probably have a talk with him before the chief finds a reason to make an arrest."

I silently prayed for that not to happen.

We came back to Lake Placid in time for a break before venturing to talk to our own persons of interest – John Peterson and Will Pratt.

"I'll see you ladies later," I said as Ann dropped us off at Ingrid's cottage.

"Three o'clock?" Nicole asked.

I nodded, waved goodbye, and walked up the stone steps. A soft light lit the porch.

Before I could unlock the door, Fritz came bounding up the steps, tail wagging and tongue hanging out.

Teddy was very glad to see him and gave a "yip" of excitement trying to pull away.

"Sorry, boy. I have your leash attached so you won't be escaping like Fritz here."

Eva walked into the yard carrying a black leash and heaved a sigh of relief.

"There you are, you naughty dog."

"I think he just wants to play."

"Hi, Jillian. It's been hard to give him the attention he needs. Gumby used to...."

"I know, I know. Why don't we let them play inside a while and I'll make us a cup of tea."

"That sounds wonderful. I'll take you up on your offer."

I went to the kitchen and put the kettle on.

Teddy and Fritz followed. After getting a drink, they playfully wrestled on the floor as I took out two mugs and found the tea bags.

"How are things going?" I asked.

"The funeral will be private. He wanted to be cremated and his ashes cast over the lake. The police have finished with their investigation."

I was surprised.

"Have they found the killer?"

"No. Mark said the only person of interest is Sam Hunt, but they only have a possible motive and an approximate time frame of him being at the scene."

"What about the weapon? I heard he was stabbed."

"Yeah, that leaked out, I know. Evidently whoever killed Gumby wiped their prints clean and put the knife back where it belonged."

"So they've proved the actual weapon used."

She nodded.

I poured the steaming water over the tea bags and set the kettle back on the stove.

"We'll let our tea steep awhile."

"How can the chief close the case if the killer isn't caught? It doesn't make sense."

"Because Mark said he's taken statements from everyone who may have been connected with Gumby and there aren't any leads. No one seems to know anything."

Perhaps the right questions weren't asked.

I removed the tea bags and offered Eva milk and sugar.

"What will you do now, Eva?"

She shook her head.

"I feel numb. Gumby was my life. I've never worked and don't have many friends. My husband was not the social type. I don't have a clue what I'm going to do."

"Where else could you go?" I sipped the tea all the while wishing for a nap.

"Lake Placid is the only home I've ever known. We bought the house when Drew hired my husband as executive chef."

"A move is difficult but a fresh start might be something to consider. What did you major in? "

"Humanities. It was the easiest major to get a degree in at Dartmouth."

"I'm sure there are careers in humanities. Working in a museum might be interesting."

"Or an art gallery. I've thought about it. What I really love is gardening, but I don't know how I'd fare at working at a garden center."

She finished her tea.

I offered a refill but she shook her head.

"I need to be getting home. There's a mountain of paperwork to do with him gone."

"I remember. But once you get organized you'll find a sense of satisfaction knowing you can care for yourself if you have to."

"I'll be glad when I reach that point. Come on Fritz, let's get home. We'll do a workout in the back yard."

Fritz pricked up his ears and marched to Eva. She attached his leash and the two said goodbye.

I found it difficult to understand Chief Taylor's closing the investigation so abruptly. It was as if he knew who the killer was and wanted to protect him....

Or her.

CHAPTER TEN

After a brief nap, I shook myself awake, combed my hair, and touched up my lipstick.

"Let's go see what we can find out from those two staffers, Teddy."

"Woof!" he barked ready for action.

The rain clouds from the morning had dispersed giving way to a clear sunshiny day.

A brisk walk led us to the front gate of the patio at The Cottage.

After installing Teddy in his tote, I gave him instructions to behave.

He looked at me with those dark brown eyes as if to say, "You bring me to a restaurant and ask me to behave with all those delicious smells in the air?"

Ann and Nicole crossed the street from the inn and joined us.

A different host seated us, took our drink orders, and handed us menus. I wondered if anyone was hungry. We'd only just had lunch.

My jeans felt a little tight.

No order for me.

"How does ice cream sound?" Ann asked.

"You ladies go ahead. I'll order a small dish for Teddy."

They both stared at me.

"I don't care what people think. You know that."

"Suit yourself." Ann seemed unruffled.

Nicole only smiled.

We watched and waited for the inn workers to appear.

I could see Sam working inside the cafe so we weren't able to talk to him.

As I sat facing the door, I saw Will Pratt enter.

"Will just walked in," I said.

"I have an idea." Ann grabbed her purse. "Every chef likes to hear compliments, right?"

Nicole and I now stared at her.

"I'll be back when I've finished with him."

I almost felt sorry for him.

The server brought a hot fudge sundae for Nicole and a dish of vanilla ice cream for Teddy.

"Will he need a spoon?" Her question held a touch of sarcasm.

"Yes, please. And could I have a cup of water?"

"Be right back."

I strained to see how Ann was doing with Will.

"She's sitting at the bar with him."

Nicole turned her head toward the gate.

"Is that the man you're looking for who just came in?"

I shifted my eyes to where she looked.

"We're in luck!" I handed Teddy in his tote to her.

"Take him a minute, would you? I'll be right back."

"Come here, sweet doggie, and let Aunt Nicole feed you your ice cream."

John Peterson was alone. He didn't have a chance.

I made my approach.

"Excuse me, but weren't you working at the front desk the other night when my friends and I came for dinner?"

"Probably. I think I remember you. You were with two other ladies, weren't you?"

"My, what a good memory you have. John, isn't it?"

"Now who has the good memory?"

"I wonder if I couldn't buy you something to drink. And a snack perhaps? A burger or one of their Artisan pizzas?"

He eyed me suspiciously.

"I am hungry."

"Well, you need to come on over to our table. I'll hail the server."

After ordering a beer and some pizza, he leaned back.

"Why do you want to talk to me? It isn't anything illegal is it?"

"Not at all," I said. "We're only interested in finding out what really happened the night Chef Gumm was murdered. Curiosity, you might say."

"I've been through all the details with the police. I heard they closed the investigation."

"You heard that, too?" Nicole asked.

"John, don't you think it strange that the investigation has stopped all of a sudden?"

He shrugged.

"I suppose the police know what they're doing. Rumor has it that it may have been someone on drugs. They may not be telling us because they're laying a trap or something."

"It's possible." I wiped Teddy's mouth with a napkin and gave him a sip of water. "Or they're trying to protect someone. Just a thought."

John looked worried.

"Now that you mention it, there was something. I didn't think it was important at the time, but now it may be."

"We're listening," I said.

"I remember being especially busy that evening. We usually are when we have live entertainment. A meeting was going on in the back dining room by the fireplace."

"When was this?" I asked.

"I think it was about 9:30 p.m. when it started. I remember because they wanted to make sure they could still get drinks before the bar closed."

"Who was at the meeting?"

"They were city councilmen. Let's see if I can remember – there was Bill Wright – he's a big tax attorney on several boards in the community, and Ron Carson."

"What does he do?" I asked.

"He's some kind of developer. I'm not sure exactly but I think it's real estate. There was an article about him not too long ago. Something about him being terminated from the company he worked for because it was bought out and they brought in their own people.

"Was there anyone else?" Nicole leaned in.

"There might have been, but those were the only ones I could see going in from the bar to the back room."

He took the last swig of beer and finished off his pizza.

"It's been nice talking to you ladies, but I have some friends waiting inside. Thanks for the beer and pizza."

He rose and left the table.

Just as he entered, Ann came out, so he held the door open. Her face held a look of victory.

"All set, ladies? I think we need to take a walk."

Once on the street, I placed Teddy on the ground and we began walking toward the boathouse a little ways down from The Cottage.

The small beach stood empty. Three Adirondack chairs on the dock beckoned for us to come and sit. As Teddy napped in my lap, we shared information.

"Will Pratt isn't the friendliest person I've ever met," Ann said. "But he was forthcoming and didn't seem to mind talking about the subject of murder."

"That's a little strange, don't you think?" Nicole asked.

"Wait until you hear what he told me – you'll really think it strange."

"We're listening," I said.

"To begin with, he thinks Sam Hunt killed Chef Gumm. Will confessed to telling the police he witnessed the parking lot fight and told them Sam was still near the kitchen when he left."

"That is damaging. At least we didn't have to tell the police what we saw." Nicole watched a duck swim past.

"It's so beautiful here," she said. "Why would anyone want to disturb such a peaceful community with murder?"

I stroked Teddy gently.

"If we knew why, as I've said before, we'd know *who*."

"Ann, did Will give any hint of a motive for him to kill Gumm?"

Ann looked thoughtful.

"The man strikes me as unfeeling. Condemning Sam in such a callous way seemed contrived as if someone else decreed it." Ann shook her head.

"I can see how it would bother you. Almost as if someone put the noose around Sam's neck," Nicole said.

"If that's true, the murderer may have carefully planned Gumm's death," I said.

"Or found an opportunity to get rid of him for some reason." Ann crossed her arms.

A breeze ruffled our hair and brought a chill, waking Teddy.

"We'd better continue our conversation at Ingrid's." I checked the time. "She'll be home by now."

"I could go for a cup of tea," Ann said.

Ingrid greeted us as we came into the cottage.

"You ladies look as if you need a cup of tea." Have a seat while I make us some."

Teddy scampered into the kitchen for a drink of water while we found comfortable places to sit in the living room.

She returned with a tray of mugs filled with steaming tea.

"Help yourself to milk and sugar."

After polite conversation of our day's travel, I turned to her.

"Have you heard anything about Sam?"

She took a sip of tea, and set the mug on a side table.

"Claire said Chief Taylor came over and had a talk with him. He was told not to leave town, which sounded ominous to me."

"I agree. Ingrid, we talked to Will Pratt and he thinks Sam killed Chef Gumm. He's the one who told the chief about seeing them argue the night of the murder."

"This is terrible!" Ingrid said.

"Now don't worry," Ann said. "We're not going to rest until we ferret out who really killed him."

"You may be able to help us with what we've learned," I said.

"Anything!"

Teddy wanted up in my lap.

"Come here, sweet dog."

Once he was settled, I patted him and continued.

"We must think back to what was going on the night Gumm was killed."

"Did you talk to John Peterson?" she asked.

"Yes, and you may be able to help us." I referred to my phone. "He gave us the names of two men he remembered who met in the private dining room."

Ann raised her eyebrows. Of course, she wasn't aware of our conversation on the patio.

"What can you tell us about Ron Carson or Bill Wright? They're city councilmen."

Ingrid looked away for a moment.

"I've heard the names or read them in the paper. Ron Carson has been to the inn before – Claire mentioned him once because he was a big shot in town and came in for dinner on occasion."

"What did she say about him?" I continued gently patting Teddy.

Ingrid furrowed her brow.

"I only remember her saying he was impatient and seemed difficult because of the way he treated his wife at the table."

"Interesting." Nicole looked thoughtful. "Maybe he was under stress about something."

"Could be. I'm sure they have offices in town – I've driven past Bill Wright's law office before."

"Good," Nicole said. "We might find out something if we pay them a visit."

"How are we going to do that?" Ann asked. "Why do you think they're going to tell us anything?"

"Jillian can think of something, can't you?" She looked at me with pleading eyes.

I thought a moment, and came up with an idea.

"If these men thought we were viable clients, they would talk to us. You know I can't lie, but I may be able to have an interest suitable to the task."

The three women sipped their tea and waited for my idea.

"The developer will be easy to talk to. All I have to say is I'm interested in buying some property for a lake house."

"Have you thought about it?" Nicole asked.

I smiled. "I did just now."

"What about the tax attorney?" Ann asked.

"That may be more difficult. No – wait!"

"You have an idea?" Ingrid asked. "I'm going to bring us more tea."

After Ann and Nicole returned to their room for a while, Claire stopped in to visit her mom.

She seemed depressed.

Ingrid insisted I join in the visit.

"How is Sam?" Ingrid asked her.

"Worried. The police are watching his every move. It's making him a nervous wreck! He can't study because he can't concentrate."

"Oh, dear," I said. "I wonder if he'll talk to me. He may be able to shed some light on what happened that night."

Claire took Teddy from the floor and held him. "He might. I'll ask him when he gets home from work tonight."

I thought about how young they were. If Sam was convicted of a murder he didn't commit both their lives would be ruined.

"You both work different shifts, am I right?"

"Sam is on call due to his class schedule. I work the dinner shift. I can't stay long."

"Claire, do you remember a meeting going on in the private dining room on the night Gumm was killed?"

She shifted her eyes.

"No meeting was scheduled. We close at 9 p.m. I remember the bar was full though, because of the live music."

"What can you remember? Any detail might be important."

"I finished my shift, and went through the hallway that leads to the kitchen to get my coat."

"What did you see?"

"The dishwasher was washing up, and Chef Pratt was putting things away – pots and pans, and food."

"Did you see Chef Gumm?"

"Yes. He was in his small office working on something – it looked like paperwork."

"Did he appear normal?"

She nodded.

"He left his desk, came over, and tried helping me on with my coat. No one could see us because the hall bends before coming into the kitchen."

"You say 'tried' – what happened?"

"I...I need to get to work. I won't forget to tell Sam you want to talk to him."

Claire was visibly upset about the incident.

Ingrid hugged her before she left.
We simply had to find the truth.

CHAPTER ELEVEN

Sam agreed to see me immediately.

Ingrid volunteered to watch Teddy and feed him if I didn't get back in time. She understood someone could be following me.

With him taken care of, I borrowed her car and went to Sam's apartment.

The Alpine Village apartment complex was located just outside of town behind a small shopping center.

I climbed three flights of stairs to reach apartment 374 and knocked.

Sam peered through a crack in the door locked with a chain.

"Just a minute," he said as he slid the lock open.

"Come on in." He moved some books and a binder off the sofa onto the kitchen table before motioning me to sit down.

"How are you holding up?" I asked.

He shrugged.

"Not too bad. I'll be glad when this is over, though."

"I can imagine it's been hard. I'd like to help."

He studied me, and sat down at the table.

"How can you help when the police have already made up their minds I'm guilty?"

I smiled.

"I have secret weapons."

He raised his eyebrows in surprise.

"You're some kind of superhero?"

I chuckled.

"I'm not, but God is."

That caught Sam's attention.

"I'm listening."

"Before I ask you some questions, I need to know the truth."

He shifted in his chair.

"Okay. You want something to drink?"

I shook my head.

Sam opened the refrigerator and took out a soda.

"Did you stab Chef Gumm in the back?" I asked.

With eyes level Sam shook his head.

"I wanted to. But I'm smart enough to know it wouldn't be worth going to prison and losing Claire if I did something stupid like that."

He popped open the soda and took a swig.

"Wise decision."

I felt relief.

"But someone killed him after you and he argued. Think hard about everything that happened – any detail might be important."

Sam sat back in the chair and tried to focus.

"I remember a car drove by just about the time Gumm hit me."

"That would have been Will Pratt."

"Yeah, that's what Chief Taylor said."

"I remember Gumm laughed at me when I fell. He walked back inside the kitchen and I picked myself up off the ground."

"What happened after that?"

"Things were quiet until I heard a noise. It came from somewhere close. I looked around and didn't see anything so I assumed it was a cat near the dumpster."

"Did you see the cat?"

"No. I was still angry so I got in my car and left."

"And that's all you saw or heard?"

"That's all I can think of."

"Sam, I asked Claire this but I'm going to ask you, too. When you went to see Gumm, what do you remember?"

He bit his lip.

"All I could think about was Claire coming home after work all upset. She was crying and shaking."

"Go on."

"She told me Gumm had made advances again – this time he was actually physical. I still get furious whenever I think about it!"

"What time was this?"

"Around 9:30 or 10 p.m. I went crazy – she tried to stop me but I was determined to tell him off."

"So you left and went to the inn. What happened next?"

"I parked in front and went through the front entrance. There weren't too many people there at that time of night."

"Whom did you see?"

"John was working the desk. There were a couple of men talking in the private dining room – some kind of meeting I guess."

"No one else?"

He shook his head.

"I walked through the hallway to the kitchen. I heard Gumm talking to someone at the back door but I couldn't tell who it was."

"What did they say? Could you hear?"

"Gumm yelled something at them like 'you've had your last chance,' and slammed the door."

"I see. And when Gumm turned around, he saw you."

Sam nodded.

"He asked what I wanted. I told him to leave Claire alone or I'd have her swear out a complaint."

"How did he react?"

"He was smug. 'Her word against mine' that's what he said, and told me to get out."

"Is that when you left?"

"No. I told him I wasn't leaving until he promised to leave Claire alone."

"And he wouldn't."

"He came at me, grabbed the back of my shirt and threw me out the back door. I stood up and yelled at him threatening to do what I'd said."

"And that's when he hit you."

Sam hung his head.

I walked over to him and put my hand on his shoulder.

"I wasn't kidding about secret weapons, Sam. I've prayed that God will help us find the killer. You must have faith that He will."

Sam looked up at me.

"Okay. It's going to take a miracle to get me out of this so yeah, okay – add me to your believer's list."

I smiled.

"Mrs. Bradley, you said secret weapons – what's the other one?"

"My garden club friends and Teddy. We're kind of like a team."

"Kind of an odd team, I'd say. But, hey, if you can find out who did this, I'll be your biggest fan!"

"I'd better be going. You have studying to do."

I nodded toward his homework.

"Yes, ma'am."

I started for the door.

"Mrs. Bradley – thanks for coming over. Can I walk you to your car?"

I chuckled.

"Thanks, but I'm not that old yet!"

"Sorry. Take care."

"You, too, Sam."

As I walked carefully down the stairs holding on to the railing, I thought I saw a shadow dart back into the hallway on the second floor.

I hurried down the last flight and turned to see if someone was lurking.

Nothing. Perhaps my imagination was getting the better of me.

The shadow reappeared.

I took the keys from my purse and held the ignition key between two fingers in case I needed a weapon to defend myself.

The only thing I heard was the crunching of my shoes on the gravel driveway where I'd parked.

Once inside the car I locked the doors and checked the rearview mirror.

Again, nothing.

When this happened before in Half Moon Bay, it was someone following me because I was getting close to finding the truth.

Was it happening again?

I drove home glancing in the rearview mirror every few seconds. It seemed a car was following me but it turned off before I turned on Main Street.

Better be careful, Jillian.

This was one time I was glad I wasn't walking from the inn to Ingrid's.

I parked in her driveway and hurried inside.

Teddy was wagging his tail and yipping, elated to see me.

I scooped him up and gave him a hug and a kiss.

Ingrid came out from the kitchen.

"He's been a good boy. He led me into the kitchen and stared at me until I fixed his supper."

"Now you see what I mean about him being psychic."

"I do. How was the visit with Sam?"

I shared what he'd told me.

She nodded appreciatively. "I was making a cup of tea. Would you like some?"

"I'd love a cup."

I followed her into the kitchen.

"I think someone may have followed me to Sam's apartment."

"Really – that's not good! Should you call the police?"

"What would I tell them? They'd probably think I was a silly old woman looking for attention. But I was scared."

"You shouldn't go out alone. Anyway, at least for now, you're home safe."

A text came in. It was from Drew.

"It looks like the girls and I have a date with Drew Olson tomorrow morning. He wants to show us the view from the ski jump."

"What about Teddy? You're not going to take him way up there are you?"

Teddy pricked up his ears when he heard his name. He cocked his head at Ingrid."

She handed me a mug of tea. I stirred in a heaping teaspoon of sugar.

"This text says Eva will watch him. I hope it won't be an imposition."

"Fritz will enjoy the company. I saw Eva this morning taking him for a walk. She doesn't look good."

"I'm sure that's normal. Grief isn't kind to one's looks. I'll go over there a little early to chat."

"It's interesting."

"What is?"

"Drew and Eva. He's been over to see her at least twice a day since it happened. I've seen his car."

"They're close, I assume."

"I'd say they were. Their mother died last year. It was strange."

"Strange? How so?"

I sipped the tea and enjoyed its warm goodness.

"From what I gathered she went crazy and jumped out her bedroom window. Her room was on the third floor of the home she was in."

"How terrible! Eva mentioned she had passed away but didn't mention how she died."

"Mrs. Olson was a formidable part of this community. She ran the inn single_handedly after her husband died – until Drew was old enough to take over."

"So now the inn belongs to Drew and Eva."

She nodded.

"More tea?"

"No thanks. I'm meeting my friends for dinner soon. May I impose on you to watch Teddy again?"

"Of course. I like the company. He must be a wonderful companion. Claire wants a dog but they're still not settled."

"Sam told me."

"Really? That's a good sign. Claire doesn't think he's listening sometimes."

"He loves her – it's obvious. Now that Gumm's dead, the harassment has stopped and they can get on with their lives."

"They do have dreams. We'll talk about the kids later. Right now you may want to freshen up before meeting your friends for dinner."

I glanced at the time.

"You're right. Thanks."

I handed Teddy to her.

"Go to Aunt Ingrid."

"And Jillian, please take my car."

I nodded that I would.

I took the elevator to Ann and Nicole's room. They'd left the door ajar.

"I'm here and I'm hungry," I said.

"Any ideas where we should go for dinner?" Ann asked.

"Anything is fine with me," Nicole said.

I sat in the big wing back chair.

"One place on Main Street caught my eye. I don't know whether it was subliminal or a catchy sign – *The Brown Dog Cafe.*"

"You were thinking of Teddy?" Ann asked.

"Of course. Shall we give it a try?"

Ann typed on her phone.

"I'll Google it for reviews."

"And check the menu," I said. "I'm hungry for steak."

Ann smiled as she handed me her phone.

"Will this do?"

A sumptuous photo of steak atop mashed potatoes sealed the deal.

We decided to walk since the cafe was close.

"Sam and I chatted this afternoon. From what he told me, there may have been another person in the parking lot during the argument."

I shared exactly what he'd said.

The Brown Dog Cafe was French cuisine. I didn't care what the cuisine was as long as I could get a steak.

We were seated at a table with a shimmering view of Mirror Lake.

The cafe was full of patrons. From the looks on their happy faces, they seemed to be enjoying their meals.

Servers placed plates of delicious looking food in front of their guests. I would be happy when it was our turn.

"This was a good choice, Jillian." Ann took a forkful of sugar seared organic Scottish Salmon. She closed her eyes in delight.

I cut my portions in two and pushed half aside.

"The filet is divine!"

Nicole selected a Meyer lemon and garlic herb roasted gulf prawn with her fork and took a bite.

She nodded approval.

"Did anyone else notice the use of farm attributions on the menu?" I asked.

The server approached with a pitcher of water.

"Excuse me," I said. "Who supplies your produce and specialty meats?"

He filled our glasses to the top.

"We have different suppliers. But we choose from the exchange to get the best quality."

"Thank you."

The server passed on to the next table.

"Jillian, what are you thinking?" Nicole asked.

"What if our friend Quincy was going to lose the inn's business for his boss?"

"From the looks of his quarters at the farm that would not be good." Ann swirled a piece of salmon in the braised grape tomato – charred lemon confit and lifted it to her mouth.

"I sing your praises for choosing this restaurant, Jillian."

"Thank you," I said as the server removed our plates and offered a dessert tray.

I had been judicious about the entrée portions.

"I'll have the Crème Caramel. Extra spoons, please."

"Perfect," Nicole said.

We all ordered cappuccinos, however. A decadent treat celebrating our getaway.

"We may not be thinking clearly regarding Quincy, if he was the one Gumm yelled at."

I offered spoons to Ann and Nicole after the server brought my dessert.

They succumbed.

"Are you saying Quincy wanted to lose the inn's business?" Ann took a bite.

"If Gumm fired them, they'd be free to join the exchange." I stirred sugar into my cappuccino and sipped the delicious brew.

"Are you suggesting Quincy was trying to get fired?" Ann asked.

"If he was, he wouldn't have a motive for killing Chef Gumm unless...." Nicole said.

"Unless Gumm drove him to it. If someone is treated badly long enough and hard enough...." I said.

"It could lead to murder."

Ann said what I was thinking.

CHAPTER TWELVE

The following morning I put on some sweats and took Teddy for a walk along the lane. We passed Eva's house, but no one stirred.

I pulled my jacket close around me in the chilly air. The wind whipped through the trees separating dead leaves from life giving branches.

Death eventually claims us all, but Eva's mother and husband died within a year. It was a double grief for her.

Teddy didn't want to go back inside, but I insisted.

"It's too cold out there!" I said.

I took off his leash and hung it on the coat rack.

Teddy sniffed breakfast coming from the kitchen where Ingrid banged pots and pans together.

"Good morning," I said. "Something smells good."

"I'm making omelets this morning. Chose whatever you like. Help yourself to coffee."

On the counter were bowls of chopped bacon, cheese, sautéed veggies, and salsa.

"Yes, please!" I said.

I waited for the omelet to cook before making Teddy's breakfast, adding bits of whole-wheat toast.

Helping myself to breakfast, I sat down to enjoy my steaming omelet, making myself at home.

Ingrid glanced out the window.

"Looks like it's going to be a beautiful day. Perfect for your visit to the ski jump."

"Honestly, I never would have chosen to ride up to a place that high, but Drew was insistent."

Teddy finished his breakfast, lapped some water, and came over to where I sat and lay by my feet.

"Drew can be persuasive. I've seen him with Eva."

"What about with her late husband?"

"I rarely saw them together. I don't think they were amicable, but Gumm didn't get along with most people."

"I wonder why. Did something bad happen to him?"

"I'm not sure. You could ask Eva."

After a second cup of coffee, I was ready to get dressed and be on my way.

"I'll see you after work," Ingrid said. "I'm leaving now. Be careful on that ski jump."

I smiled weakly.

Eva did not look well when she answered the door.

"Are you sure you still want to watch Teddy?" I asked.

She merely nodded.

"It gives me an excuse to stay home and not have to get dressed. Come in."

"I can relate."

In spite of Eva not looking well her house was neat and tidy, which gained my respect.

Fritz rushed up to greet Teddy. Tails wagged and the wrestling commenced.

"They'll have a good time together," she said.

The doorbell rang.

Eva looked surprised.

"Were you expecting company?" I asked.

She answered the door.

It was Chief Taylor holding coffee from Starbucks and a small sack.

Now it was his turn to look surprised.

"Oh I'm sorry. I didn't realize you had company."

"Jillian is on her way out. Come in. Drew is taking her to see the ski jump."

"I see." He handed her the sack. "I brought those scones you like."

"That was so nice of you." She took the sack and invited him in. "Starbucks sounds perfect – I haven't had breakfast."

"Well, I'd better be going," I said.

"Jillian – be careful today." The chief sounded sincere. "People have been hurt on that thing."

"I'm not actually going down the jump, Chief."

What I *wanted* to say but didn't was, "Nice to see you working today."

"Thanks again for watching Teddy, Eva. I'll be back as soon as I can, and we can have a chat."

She smiled and closed the door.

So much for my loneliness theory.

The brisk walk down to the inn felt good. Fog hovered along the shore, skimming the lake. A few swimmers were out with a lone canoe.

The church bell rang, transporting me once again to the uniqueness of this beautiful part of the country.

Murder, however, was not unique. Motives were different, but murder meant a life taken by someone who wanted that life out of the way.

Who wanted Eva's husband out of the way?

Before I had a chance to try to answer my own question, I looked up and saw my friends standing in the parking lot with Drew Olson.

They all waved when they saw me.

I suppose I couldn't turn back now. It would be too embarrassing.

"Ready, ladies?" Drew opened the car doors for us. Ann and Nicole settled in the back seat, conspicuously leaving me the front.

Drew beamed. "Be prepared for an unforgettable experience. Whenever I go up the mountain, I still get a rush."

The only rush I felt was my heart sending extra blood flow to my veins.

We reached the base of Whiteface Mountain ski jump area where Drew graciously bought our tickets.

"This was my idea so it's my treat." Drew led the way to the ski lift.

"We'll take our own car," Ann said. "You and Drew ride in the next one."

Thanks, Ann – forever the matchmaker.

Drew put the holding bar down and the ride to the top of the mountain began.

"Does this bring back memories?" Conversation might diffuse the fact that we would be traveling in an open car hanging by a single wire to the base of a ski jump.

"It does. I've ridden this lift hundreds of times training for the Olympics."

"Your medal is impressive. I read the magazine article at Ingrid's."

"Those were my glory days. Still, one must move ahead."

I wondered what he meant by that.

"I still love to ski. The inn takes most of my time, though, especially in the winter. That's our peak season."

"You have good staff. Can't you delegate and do some skiing?"

"Yes and no. Skiing takes an entire day. I'm always putting out fires, as they say. Now I have to deal with finding a head chef."

"Isn't Chef Pratt qualified?"

"No. He's doing a good job but an executive chef has to have higher qualifications than Will has."

"Chef Gumm was a fine chef. We enjoyed the one meal he prepared. What a tragedy for Eva."

"She'll be okay. Eva's a good person. Who knows? She may even marry again."

I said nothing.

We were half way up the mountain. Drew was right – the views were spectacular in spite of hating the way the wind blew my hair.

Ann and Nicole turned occasionally to wave.

Little schemers!

We arrived at the top. Drew helped me out of the lift chair. It was good to be on solid ground again.

"The elevator is this way." Drew put his hand on my back to guide me. A bit flirtatious, but I didn't mind. It was nice to have someone show protection.

The top of the tower above us stood 253 feet. Even the views from the bottom were fantastic. Now I couldn't wait to see what they were like from the ski platform.

"What do you think so far?" Drew asked as we stepped into the glass elevator.

Nicole shook her head.

"There's really no way to describe it. Almost like a bird's eye view hovering over the world."

"Spectacular views, Drew." Ann pointed to a smaller jump area. "What are they doing?"

"Those are junior athletes practicing flips and turns in the artificial snow. They'll land in the swimming pool when they're finished."

I could see the fond recollections in his eyes.

"Now I'll show you something scary."

I stood behind Ann.

"Chicken," Nicole whispered.

The view was steeper than any roller coaster ride I'd ever taken. Drew was right – it was terrifying to think of skiers speeding down with an initial take-off speed of 60 miles per hour.

"Well, that's the show, ladies." Drew held the elevator door while we entered. "How does lunch sound?"

"Can you spare the time?" I asked.

"Ingrid is covering for me."

"Where do you suggest?" Ann asked.

Milano North above Starbucks proved to be a perfect lunch choice. Drew certainly knew his way around, but why wouldn't he? He had lived here his whole life.

He waved to the chef preparing food in the open kitchen.

The chef nodded in return.

"You'll enjoy this chef's cuisine. I wish I could hire him away."

"Lunch is on me, I insist." I gave a look of determination.

One look at the menu and I knew I was in trouble.

I glanced at Drew.

"I'm going to splurge and take the leftovers home. The temptation is too hard to resist."

He seemed pleased.

I placed my order for a cup of cream of asparagus soup and homemade rigatoni `a la vodka with leeks and mushrooms. For dessert, I chose the olive oil cake with citrus ricotta mousse and velvety limoncello sauce.

I was not disappointed.

"Coffee?" Drew asked. "*My treat.*"

He knew how to reach me.

My friends tried to hide their smiles but were unsuccessful.

"I should probably rescue Eva from Teddy." I placed my napkin beside my plate and paid the check.

"I should be getting back, too." Drew helped me out of my chair.

He either was flirting or considered me frail. I chose to think the former.

We rode in silence during the short trip back to the inn. Drew dropped Ann and Nicole off and insisted on driving me to Eva's.

"I'd like to walk you to the door, but I really should get back to work."

He was charming.

"There's no need. Thanks for a wonderful time." I patted his hand. "I'm glad you talked me into going."

"It was my pleasure. See you for dinner?"

"We'll see."

I stepped out of the car, and walked to Eva's door.

He waited until I was safely inside before he left.

I liked that.

Thoughts of Vincent began to fade. How could I have a serious relationship with a man on a different continent? I had to stop kidding myself.

Drew was charming but also tied to the inn. I recalled winter photos I'd seen in one of the brochures and could understand never wanting to leave.

The dogs yipped from inside hearing my knock. Eva held them back as I squeezed in the door."

Teddy couldn't wait for me to pick him up.

"Did you and Fritz have fun while I was gone?"

"Woof!" he barked.

Never was there a cuter dog.

He wriggled free and joined Fritz sprawled on the floor.

"Would you like some tea?" Eva asked. "I was going to make me a cup." She headed for her kitchen.

Even though I'd had coffee, a cup of tea would give us a chance to chat.

"I'd love one, thanks." I took a seat on the sofa.

Eva did seem in need of company.

She returned to the living room, handed me a cup and napkin, and sat in an overstuffed chair.

"What did you think of our ski jump?"

"The views were phenomenal. I now have a better appreciation for what our winter athletes go through to reach the Olympics."

"Drew loved them."

"I gathered that." I sipped the sweet hot tea. "How's the investigation going? Did Chief Taylor bring any news this morning?"

Eva blushed.

"No. He only stopped by to check on me."

"I think he's fond of you. Did he ever marry?"

"Gale died of cancer. She was pretty young. They had no children. He never met anyone else after she was gone."

"That's awful."

"We're good friends, as you may have noticed."

I smiled.

"I understand. I have a friend like that at the moment. For a long time I believed we were in love, but something happened."

Eva regarded me.

"What went wrong?"

"I wish I knew."

"Eva, I might as well tell you that my friends and I want to help find your husband's killer."

She looked astonished.

"Why? You didn't even know Gumby."

"No, but we think the chief suspects Sam Hunt."

"Is this Claire's husband?"

I nodded. "And Ingrid's son-in-law."

"I see. So you're doing this for her sake."

"And for Claire's. She and Sam are so young. Deep down I don't think Sam killed him."

"But what if he did?"

"At least we will have tried to help all we could."

"I like Ingrid. She's been a good employee and a wonderful neighbor. If I can help, I will."

"I was hoping you would. It's what we really want, isn't it?

"To find the truth."

CHAPTER THIRTEEN

Eva and I sipped our tea and chatted while the dogs slept peacefully on the floor.

I needed to find out answers to nagging questions.

"Eva, did your husband ever work for anyone else as an executive chef?" I asked casually.

"No." She shifted in her chair. "He started in Austria working his way up from dishwasher to sous chef in a restaurant in Salzburg."

"I thought I detected an accent."

"There was an incident. Gumby lost his job and came to the United States. He found work with a caterer who did a party for my mother."

"Yes, I remember you mentioned that."

"Anyway, he couldn't get anywhere with the catering job so he went to school at night until he passed the requirements for executive chef."

"How admirable."

"Sadly, no one would hire him."

"Because of his record?"

She nodded.

"The head chef in Salzburg took credit for one of Gumby's recipes. It made him mad and Gumby hit him – hard. The chef was hospitalized and pressed charges."

"And made sure no one would ever hire him."

Eva nodded.

"It almost destroyed him. After all his hard work."

"But he was hired at the inn."

"Drew said he'd bring him on as Executive Chef and promised he would always have a job, as long as the inn stayed in the family."

"What about this exchange I heard about?"

Eva's eyes flickered.

"Who told you about the exchange?"

"We talked to Quincy Morgan when we visited the farmers market. Why was there such an aversion to it?"

"Gumby tried to keep costs down the best he could. The exchange almost guaranteed food prices would escalate."

"But what about the other restaurants? Surely, they would balk at paying steeper prices, especially to non-exchange members."

"They had no choice. Gumby had an iron clad contract that promised Hunt's exclusivity in exchange for fair prices."

"Will that change now?"

"I'm not sure. It may depend on who becomes Executive Chef or the contract. Gumby didn't like to talk much about work when we were together."

Eva had a faraway look about her.

I gave her a moment.

"Chef Pratt seems to be taking things in stride. Did he and your husband get along?"

She hesitated a moment before answering.

"We never talked about him. I suppose they worked okay together. The only person he mentioned was that Quincy Morgan you talked to."

"I almost felt sorry for him. His living conditions were substandard."

"Farmers are not paid enough. But neither are head chefs unless you're famous.

"How about more coffee?"

"Oh, no thanks. I should be going soon. Eva, are you aware of the reason Chief Taylor suspects Sam Hunt of killing your husband?"

She hung her head. When she lifted it again, her eyes filled with tears.

"Jillian, I know the rumors. And they may be true but it doesn't matter. I know Gumby loved me."

I stood up and put my arm around her shoulder.

"I'm sure he did, Eva. No husband is perfect."

"It was all show with him. A need for attention. Mine wasn't enough although I did the best I could."

"Some men are never satisfied. Did you ever seek counseling for his behavior?"

She laughed bitterly.

"Once. When he found out I'd gone to get help from our Bishop, he hit me - and not only once. After that, I never mentioned it again."

I shook my head, truly sorry for her.

"But Jillian, you need to know it was the only time he lost control with me. It was years ago when he first started his job at the inn."

"Thanks for being open with me. I apologize for having to probe - reopening wounds. It's all in the past now."

Teddy stretched and came to me.

It's as if he was saying, "I'm ready to go home now and have my supper."

I scooped him up and hugged him.

The church bell chimed marking five o'clock.

"I'd better get back – Teddy needs his dinner. Thanks for the coffee. And thanks for watching him."

"Thanks for the company. It's good to talk. I hope you'll come again."

Ingrid was bustling about in her kitchen preparing dinner, reminding me what a long afternoon it had been. The aroma of bacon and sweet onion made me hungry.

"There you are. I wondered when you'd get home."

"I've been chatting with Eva. Teddy needs his supper."

I went to the fridge and pulled out his turkey, veggies, and rice. A pinch of cheese and a few pieces of fruit completed his meal.

He waited until I'd refreshed his water before eating.

"You're some dog."

Ingrid smiled as she stirred the soup she'd prepared.

"I thought clam chowder and sourdough bread sounded good for tonight. There's plenty if you and your friends want to join me."

It was a temptation.

"Are you sure you have plenty?"

"I made a double batch just in case."

My phone rang. I thought it may have been Ann or Nicole but I didn't recognize the number.

"Jillian, it's Drew. I need a favor."

"Of course, how can I help?"

"There's blight in my garden and I can't figure out what it is. I thought you might know what it is so I took a chance and bought the ingredients to make dinner as a trade-out."

"You're not working tonight?"

"After our conversation in the ski lift, I decided to take it easier. Please say you'll come. I can pick you up in ten minutes."

Ingrid cast a questioning glance.

I mouthed "Drew" and shrugged.

She smiled and nodded, as if telling me she approved.

"Okay. I'll see you in ten minutes."

"Please save me some chowder. It will make a great lunch tomorrow."

"No problem. A date with Drew, huh?"

"He has a garden issue. I'd better touch up."

"What about Teddy?"

He stared at me with ears perked.

"I think I'll take him."

"Insurance?"

"Something like that."

Instinctively, Teddy wagged his tail as if he knew he'd be coming with me.

I picked up my phone and sent Ann a text.

Drew arrived within no time, smiling as Ingrid stood by the door. He observed Teddy in my arms then spoke to her.

"Can't Teddy stay with you this evening?"

"Sorry, Mr. Olson. I'm going to visit Claire tonight. She's invited me for dessert."

I wondered if she concocted the story for my sake.

He looked rather disappointed but put a game face on.

"Shall we?" He held the door for Teddy and me.

Teddy curled in my lap as I held him in the front seat.

Drew backed carefully down the driveway and turned onto Mirror Lake Drive.

The sunset cast beautiful reflections of clouds in stunning purples and oranges over the lake.

Twinkling lights outlined the inn and outbuildings now that it was evening.

"How am I supposed to see blight in the dark?" I asked playfully.

"I've thought of that. We can bring samples inside and have a look under the lights."

"I suppose that would work. Ingrid said gardening was your hobby. Have you taken a sample to a nursery to have it checked out?"

"No time. With all this police business, I've barely had time to run errands, let alone tend my garden. I do love it, though. It gives me peace of mind."

I wondered what his issues were.

"I take it you're single."

He smiled.

"Unfortunately, marriage and I don't mix. Both divorces may have been my fault, who knows?"

"Marriage usually takes two. I'm sorry they didn't work."

"What about you, Jillian?"

Teddy shifted in my lap.

I stroked him gently and rubbed his ears to keep him calm.

"My first husband died years ago in Vietnam. A war hero. I never thought I'd marry again. We were so much in love."

"I'm sorry." He sounded quite sincere.

"I almost found happiness again last year but it was short lived. It's an unpleasant memory."

"Then we don't need to talk about it."

I nodded gratefully.

We pulled into a ranch style house on a wooded lot.

Drew took Teddy, helped me out of the car, and escorted me to the front door.

Teddy seemed to like him, and gave him a lick on the hand.

"I think he approves." Drew handed Teddy back, unlocked the front door, and ushered us inside.

A soaring rock fireplace met with a vaulted wood ceiling. The interior was comfortably furnished, typical for a bachelor, or in Drew's case a collection of hodge-podge from being twice divorced.

"I'll show you the sample and start dinner. The garden is right this way." He led me through the dining room out into a glass sunroom with great views.

"You have a conservatory like mine." I said missing my house a little now that I'd practically bequeathed it to Walter and Cecilia.

"The garden is in back. I'll show you." He opened a side door and we walked outside.

"Drew, this is lovely. You must love living here."

"It's not too bad. I don't spend enough time in my garden, as you can see." He nodded toward the petunia bed.

"Oh, dear. This is a problem." I reached down and plucked a curled, dark brown infected leaf. "Petunias are part of the nightshade family. This is probably potato blight."

"The blight associated with the potato famine in Ireland?"

"One in the same. Do you grow belladonna and brugmansia as well?"

Drew raised his eyebrows.

"In English, please."

"Amaryllis? Angel trumpet?"

"No. I assume they're also varieties of nightshade?"

I nodded.

"I'm impressed, Jillian. I need to put the touches on dinner. Let's go back inside, shall we?"

Teddy couldn't wait to explore his new environment. After Drew closed the door, Teddy wriggled free and raced off.

"Don't worry about him – he can't hurt anything." Drew went to the kitchen, washed his hands, and opened the refrigerator.

"What would you care to drink? I have just about everything."

"I bet you don't have cranberry juice."

"Ah, but I do."

I was pleasantly surprised. "You really do have everything. First, I need to wash my hands after handling blight."

"I'll show you the powder room."

As I started back down the hall, I noticed Drew's diploma. From the year he graduated, it appeared we were about the same age.

Aromas of garlic and onion filled the air when I walked into the kitchen.

"Smells good."

"Hope you like pasta."

"Adore it."

Teddy trotted into the room and sniffed.

"Teddy likes pasta, too."

We chuckled as my sweet dog kept his eyes on Drew.

"This is a recipe for Penne Pomodori Secchi. Penne tossed with grilled chicken and sun dried tomatoes in a creamy garlic Alfredo sauce." He poured wine over the chicken as it grilled in the skillet, added the penne to a pot of boiling water, and stirred.

"Grab some plates and silverware in the cupboard and drawer next to the dishwasher." He nodded the directions.

After pulling out my chair, Drew set plates of pasta and salad on the table and took a seat.

Teddy stood at attention by my feet, waiting for a sample.

I silently thanked the Lord for the food, and offered Teddy the first bite of chicken.

"Drew, this is amazing! Did you ever cook for either wife?"

He chuckled.

"No. Maybe I should have!"

The meal was delicious – better than at The View up at the inn.

"Drew, why did you ask me over tonight?"

He smiled shyly.

"Guess I'm a sucker for blondes."

"I suppose in such a small town as Lake Placid, there aren't many prospects."

His face fell at my comment.

"I'm sorry," I said. "I'm not good at taking compliments. Let's change the subject."

"Okay. You first."

"Tell me about your mom. Eva said she passed away last year."

The atmosphere seemed to grow chilly.

I waited, took several bites of the fabulous pasta, and continued feeding Teddy tiny samples.

"Mother's death was most unfortunate. We're still not clear what happened."

"My mother is approaching ninety. They do have issues with aging."

"Our mother declined rapidly. Eva and I didn't realize how fast she was going downhill with Alzheimer's until one of the orderlies mentioned it."

"What did the nursing home tell you happened?"

"The attendant gave her medication, made sure there was a glass of water on the nightstand, turned on the nightlight and left."

"Was the door closed?"

He seemed to tense.

"I'm not sure. Why do you ask?"

"No reason. I'm just trying to create a picture in my head."

"No one heard a thing afterward. Not until someone screamed when mom jumped from the window."

I paused a moment sympathetic to how he must have felt when he heard this.

"The window wasn't locked?"

He shook his head.

"It was supposed to be. The attendant swears he checked it before he left."

"Drew, I'm so sorry. Did Chief Taylor conduct an investigation?"

"Of sorts. But since mother had Alzheimer's, it appeared she took her own life. They couldn't prove otherwise. She'd always been headstrong."

"And now George is dead...."

"Was that his name?"

He nodded.

"Eva called him Gumby but no one else dared. How about dessert? I bought Tiramisu."

"If you have coffee to go with it."

He smiled.

"Will a cappuccino do?"

"I'd love one."

He rose, carried our empty plates to the kitchen, and took the Tiramisu from the refrigerator.

"I don't know how I ever lived without my cappuccino maker. It won't take long since it makes two at a time."

"Did George get along with your mother?"

He shook his head.

"She never liked him. Told him to his face she was going to fire him. I have to hand it to him, though. He still visited her in the nursing home when he found a chance."

"Did she give a reason why she didn't like him?"

"Mother called him a black sheep."

I thought of my conversation with Eva about her husband being fired in Salzburg as I sipped the perfectly frothed cappuccino.

"I'm sorry there was animosity. Eva seemed to love him."

He shook his head sadly as if to say, "If you only knew."

CHAPTER FOURTEEN

"So how do we treat the blight?" Drew asked.

Obviously, he wanted to change the course of conversation. Talking about death was depressing, I agreed.

"The first thing to do is remove the infected plants – carefully. I wouldn't use a chemical treatment because the infection more than likely came from a rogue source."

"I'll yank it out tomorrow. I'm taking the day off."

"What about the inn?"

"I'm only a text away if John needs me."

"John Peterson?"

Drew looked surprised.

"You don't miss a thing, do you?"

I merely smiled.

"Drew, I realize this is still talking about death, but I'm curious. Who do you think killed your brother-in-law?"

He shrugged, and took a sip of his cappuccino.

"It's a mystery to me. But the stabbing makes it personal. They must have had a strong reason."

"Did you find the body?"

"Yeah, unfortunately. Quincy couldn't get in the back door to the kitchen because it was locked. He came around to the front desk and asked us to let him come through."

"No one else was in the kitchen, I assume, or they would've let him in through the back."

"It was early."

"Was there a sign of a struggle?"

He considered.

"No. The kitchen was in order. Quincy asked me to find the delivery checklist. He wanted to bring his goods inside."

"Did you try to call Gumm to see where he was?"

He shook his head.

"Why not?"

"It seems surreal now. His cell phone was on his desk. I got a chill – a feeling something wasn't right."

"I'm getting goose bumps."

"I asked John at the front desk for the key to the freezer."

"And that's when you found the body."

"Quincy and I went in. The freezer curves around to the back – and there he was, lying face down with a wound in his back."

"What about the weapon?"

"We didn't see one. All the knives in the kitchen were accounted for. The killer must have put it back or taken it.

"I asked Quincy to call 911. I was too shaken. All I wanted was to get out of there and get some fresh air."

Drew seemed detached sitting there, not moving.

I reached across and patted his hand.

"Do you know if the police are calling it a murder or a homicide?"

"What difference does it make? Gumm is dead."

"It might make a difference to the killer. If it was not premeditated – say the result of an argument – it would be a homicide and may not be as punishable."

"Jillian, are you suggesting someone at the inn killed him?"

"Don't you think it's entirely possible?"

Drew seemed detached.

"I suppose. Why are you so interested in this? I thought you only cared about gardening."

I smiled.

"Let's just say over the years I've stumbled over more bodies than I care to count!"

Drew raised his eyebrows.

"You fascinate me."

I needed to redirect his attention.

"Okay, I'll drop the subject. Let me help with the dishes. I'll need to get home afterward."

"Teddy?"

I nodded.

"He'll need his walk."

"Guests are not permitted to clean up. Let's sit outside on the porch."

"I don't sit outside at night unless I have bug spray. The insects would eat me alive!"

"We can sit in the atrium."

"I really need to get Teddy home if you don't mind. It's been a lovely evening, Drew. Thank you for dinner."

"It's been a lovely day *and* evening for me, well most of it."

"I understand."

"I'll take you home."

After taking my sleepy little companion for a short walk before going inside, I found Ingrid waiting up in the living room in her robe and slippers.

"How was your evening?" She set aside a magazine she was reading and focused her attention on me.

"It was nice. Drew is a wonderful cook. He made Pomodori Secchi – penne with sun-dried tomatoes, chicken, and a garlic Alfredo sauce."

"Oh, my. You should have brought me some!" She chuckled.

Teddy looked at me with tired little eyes.

"Did you go see Claire?"

"Yes. The police are being quiet. With Sam on the suspect list, the kids are nervous."

"I hope Chief Taylor is making progress on the investigation. He may have leads he doesn't want anyone to know about."

"Let's hope so. Have you and your friends made any progress?"

I rocked Teddy in my arms like a baby.

"We want to talk to those councilmen. The sooner the better. Speaking of, I need to put Teddy to bed and get a bath."

"I'm heading to bed now myself. See you in the morning at breakfast."

"Goodnight, Ingrid. Come along, Teddy. Time for bed."

What would I do without my precious pet?

I lay his limp little body at the foot of the bed.

His little eyes closed, fast asleep.

After a hot bubble bath and a spritz of perfume, I turned off the light and climbed under the soft covers.

Even with Teddy close so I wouldn't be alone, it was hard to relax. I turned from side to side until comfortable.

As the soft glimmer of moonshine fell across the quilt, Vincent sprang to mind. What would he be thinking about as he drifted off to sleep?

Lord, please comfort Vincent's heart for whatever is bothering him. Give him strength to cope. Let him lean on You.

Handing my concern over to God helped me fall asleep.

The pleasant aroma of coffee woke me the next morning.

I swung my legs over the side of the bed and slipped on my leopard print slippers.

Teddy poked up his head at the foot of the bed. He stretched his paws, and shook himself from sleep.

"Good morning, sweet dog."

He wagged his tail, and came to me.

I gave him gentle hugs, and rubbed his ears.

With a quick kiss on top of his head, I threw on some jeans, a turtleneck and grabbed a sweater out of the closet.

"Ready for a walk this morning?"

"Woof!" he barked.

I peered out the window at the fog rolling along the banks of the lake. I watched a moment as a brave soul swam by.

It made me shiver.

"Morning, Jillian. Sleep okay?" Ingrid took out freshly baked cinnamon rolls from the oven.

She would be the death of my weight control system yet.

"I slept great. We'll be right back after a walk."

The weather was colder this morning. A stiff breeze carried masses of dead leaves to the ground.

I pulled my sweater close as Teddy led the way down to the fishing pier.

Mirror Lake was an idyllic setting. Quiet, peaceful, full of natural beauty, and yet a killer was still at large.

Ann sent a text:

We'll be ready at 9 a.m. Pick you up at Ingrid's.

I glanced at the time – I only had an hour.

Teddy finished sniffing every nook and cranny on the deck and was ready to leave.

We hiked back up the hill and went inside – more than ready for coffee and breakfast.

"Whew!" I hung my wrap on the coat rack along with Teddy's leash and followed the aroma of cinnamon to the kitchen.

"I gave Teddy fresh water. He's always so thirsty after a walk." Ingrid reached down and stroked him as he went to his bowl.

"Thanks. I'll help myself to coffee."

"And have a few cinnamon rolls. They're small."

"Right."

I took a couple so I wouldn't hurt her feelings.

"I'm meeting Ann and Nicole at 9 a.m. We're going to pay visits to the councilmen this morning."

"What happened with Drew last night?"

"We talked about his mother, how she died. So strange, don't you think, Ingrid, for a patient to be able to jump from a window of a nursing home?"

"It was bizarre. I remember how shocked the staff was when we heard. It was so unexpected, like something a crazy person would do."

"She sounded border line to me. Did the family press charges of neglect against the home?"

"Apparently not. Drew is on the board of directors so it would be like suing himself, wouldn't you think?"

I *was* thinking.

"I'm sorry. I went away for a moment. You gave me an idea, though."

"I did? Huh."

She glanced at the clock, unfastened her apron, and threw up her hands.

"I have to go to work. I'm almost late! Put the rolls away for me, please."

"No problem – I'll clean up. I'll see you this afternoon."

As I cleared the table, something about Mrs. Olson's demise didn't feel right. If she held the purse strings of Mirror Lake Inn, her death may have benefited Drew or Eva.

Or both.

"Come on, Teddy."

I scooped him up and carried him to my room.

"We need to get ready for the day."

With makeup applied, hair teased a little on top and sprayed with a little hairspray, I was ready to face the day.

Here we go, Lord. Please go before us and guide our path. Amen.

After locking the cottage, Teddy and I waited on the porch for Ann and Nicole. Sitting in the Adirondack chairs overlooking the garden was a special treat.

Ann and Nicole were right on time.

Teddy and I settled in the backseat and off to town we went.

"Drop me off at   Bill Wright's office. Remember I said I had an idea?"

Ann looked in the rear view mirror. "I remember, but you never told us what it was."

"I did some checking and found Wright gives a free 30 minute consultation if you make an appointment."

Nicole turned around.

"You actually made an appointment. That's brilliant. Did you say what for?"

"I'll tell you later."

"Wright's office is up ahead." Nicole consulted her iPhone.

I gathered my purse and put Teddy in his tote. "Nicole, you and Ann see what you can learn from Ron Carson."

"What are we supposed to say?" Nicole asked.

"Be creative. Tell him you're interested in buying a timeshare or something."

"But we'll be together," Ann said. "Won't that look funny?"

"Not if you mention you're on a girls' getaway."

"Okay, at least it's plausible."

"Good luck, Jillian."

"Thanks. I'll text when I'm finished. Be thinking of a nice place for lunch, ladies."

I smiled at my dear friends. How fortunate I was to have had their help solving cases over the years.

Ann let us out at the curb in front of a red-shingled building. A dark green awning sheltered two storefront cafes while a sandwich board advertised Bill Wright's Tax Office on the second floor.

There was no receptionist, only a clean-cut man in a plaid shirt wearing horn rimmed glasses and a nice smile sitting at a desk.

He stood as I entered and extended his hand.

"I'm Bill Wright."

"Jillian Bradley. Thank you for seeing me."

"Please have a seat." He gestured to a chair in front of his desk.

"Thank you."

His gaze went to Teddy.

"Who's your little friend?"

I took Teddy out of his tote.

"This is Teddy, my little companion."

"Woof!" Teddy barked.

Bill smiled.

"May I pet him?"

"Let him smell your hand first. That way he won't bite. Yorkies can be ferocious if you're not careful."

Teddy wagged his tail as the lawyer gave him a pat.

"How can I help you, Mrs. Bradley?"

"Jillian will be fine." I tucked Teddy back inside his tote and set him on the floor next to my chair.

"I'm staying at the Mirror Lake Inn where your name came up."

He looked surprised.

"Oh? In what context was I mentioned? I hope it was good."

"Just a passing comment."

I didn't want to give away too much.

The lawyer consulted his computer screen.

"You asked for a consultation regarding a transfer of title. Is this for your home?"

Teddy gave a small sigh and settled inside his tote for his morning nap.

Wright listened as I explained the living situation with Walter and Cecilia."

"In all due respect, Jillian, I would keep the title in your name. People's situations change. Your estate should remain safely protected if they were to divorce or experience another life change."

"Thank you. That's excellent advice. I'll keep things the way they are for the present."

I stood to leave with my purse in one hand and Teddy's tote in the other.

"Lake Placid is such a lovely little town."

I gestured to a photo hanging on his wall of the Whiteface Club and Resort.

"Do you own this resort?" I asked.

"I'm a partner in several entities. Our daughter is getting married there in the spring."

"Congratulations."

"Why do you ask?"

"Oh, I don't know. Just curious. I heard you are on the city council."

The look on his face was dark.

CHAPTER FIFTEEN

Bill Wright shifted in his chair.

"You said you were staying at Mirror Lake Inn."

I sat back down and waited.

The trap had been sprung.

"Yes. Actually, I'm staying with a friend who is on staff there. Her place is up on the lake not too far."

He shook his head and put his hands together.

"Terrible business about their head chef being murdered. I was *shocked* at the stabbing."

"It was a horrendous act. I'm next door to his widow."

"Eva?"

"She's taking it pretty hard. Do you know her?"

"I know her brother, Drew. Excuse me."

He made a voice memo. "Send flowers to Eva Gumm."

"Now, what were you saying, Jillian?"

"Nothing really. They haven't arrested anyone yet for his murder...Wait. I remember now where I heard your name."

He stared at me.

"You also look familiar. Were you there that night? In the bar?"

I pointed my finger at him.

"You were sitting with another man at a table in the corner, weren't you?"

"Good eye. That was Ron Carson. A real character – loves to kid around. Not a bad guy, though. He's married with two kids and serves with me on the city council."

"What a coincidence."

He looked at me with a glint in his eye.

"So is that why you're really here? Are you interested in Ron? I know he was interested in *you* that night."

I couldn't help blushing.

"Not exactly. I'm more interested in the meeting you had in the private dining room on the night of the murder."

"Are you some kind of detective?"

"Of sorts. Now, would you tell me about the meeting?"

"It depends on how you'll use the information."

A typical lawyer response.

"I understand about boards talking about issues outside of official meetings. But I promise it's not my intention to blow any whistles."

"If I have your word on that, ask anything you like. But I can still deny having this conversation."

"Agreed."

"You have ten minutes."

I was starving after the conversation with Bill Wright.

When Ann picked us up, I glanced briefly up at the office where I'd been.

Bill was watching us from one of the windows.

Had I stirred the waters?

"Food! I need food!"

Teddy popped up from his tote. He perked up his ears and let out a "Woof!"

"Food?" he seemed to say. "Did you mention food, mistress?"

I love this dog. Our appetites were much alike.

A restaurant sign caught my eye.

"Let's try this one." I pointed to the Chalet on the right hand side of the road with red umbrellas on the patio.

Nicole studied the site.

"It must be part of the Golden Arrow Lakeside Resort. It appears to be connected."

Ann turned into the parking lot of *Generations*, filled to capacity.

"A packed lot is always a good sign." I turned to Teddy. "Let's hope they'll let you in."

He ducked down as if he understood what to do.

Ann shook her head.

"You're going to try and sneak him in?"

"Hey. If they don't ask, I won't tell."

We chuckled.

The restaurant decor was expectantly cozy and warm with hardwood floors, walls painted a brick color, and a fire burning in the modern rock hearth.

"A booth, please."

Teddy stayed at the bottom of his tote like a good dog.

The host asked us to wait a moment. She didn't seem to notice Teddy.

"This way, please."

Good. We were in!

I sat him on the floor under the table.

"Not a peep out of you," I said to him. "I'll keep some leftovers for you later."

A different server came to our table.

"Would you ladies care to enjoy service on our patio? I noticed there's a dog."

Busted!

Without a word, our party moved to a table outside.

"The weather is lovely. We might as well enjoy it." Ann was the group's optimist.

Over a tasty Reuben, one of my favorite sandwiches of all time, Ann reported the visit to Ron Carson.

"The man almost sold me a timeshare." Ann took a bite of her Caprese salad on a bed of locally raised produce.

"I wonder where their produce comes from." Nicole filled a leaf of Boston lettuce with spicy chicken and accompaniments for her wrap.

"It's not on the menu." I wiped the corner of my mouth with a napkin, broke off a piece of melted Swiss cheese, and offered it to Teddy.

He gratefully accepted in a polite manner. A ploy to encourage more of the same.

"Generations may be part of the exchange." I took up my sandwich again.

"Carson was uncomfortable when I mentioned him being on the city council." Ann consumed the last bite of salad, and called for the dessert menu.

Nicole leaned back.

"I don't know why since he has a plaque on the wall advertising the fact. But I agree – he did seem wary."

"Did he recognize you from the bar the night Gumm was killed? I ask because Bill Wright recognized me."

"No. He didn't bring it up." Ann studied the desserts. "What he *did* say was there were three people at the meeting."

"Three?" I asked. "That is interesting."

"The third person was also on the city council." Nicole smiled. "Drew Olson."

"Drew? He never mentioned he was a member." I felt confused. Why had no one mentioned it?

"Ladies, let's think about this a minute. What is the business of city councils?"

Nicole and Ann looked at each other.

"Is this a trick question, Jillian?" Ann asked.

"Seriously. Don't city councils make decisions regarding the economic welfare of the city? At least I think they still do."

Teddy growled for more food.

I tossed him a piece of rye bread.

"Nicole, we need your computer skills help here."

She gave an innocent look.

"Moi? Just kidding, Jillian. What do you want me to find out?"

"You could take a look at recent agendas and see if anything looked interesting." I gave Teddy a spoonful of water from my glass.

"Corned beef makes me thirsty."

"What should I look for?" Nicole was immediately on her phone. "I can find out more on my computer when I get back to the room."

"Good. Ann, was there anything else of interest when you talked to Carson?"

She considered.

"There was one condo on the lake."

"Oh, stop!" I said. "Did you decide on a dessert?"

She set the menu aside.

"There's a Ben & Jerry's we passed coming in. It's not too far."

"Ice cream sounds good." Nicole signed her bill.

Teddy cocked his head.

"I know, I know. I'll get you some, don't worry."

Ann and Nicole shook their heads.

"You are crazy, Jillian." Ann took out her keys.

The neighborhood was quiet when I returned to Ingrid's cottage. Ice cream after the Reuben may have been overkill.

I unlocked the door and carried Teddy inside. He'd made a pit stop on Main Street after Ben & Jerry's, so we were good to go.

The bed offered too great a temptation. A nap would be good for us both.

After slipping off my shoes, I set Teddy on his towel.

He crashed.

I simply dozed.

The day had been productive. We'd learned that Drew was at the secret council meeting on the night Gumm was killed.

It may have been nothing, but my spirit sensed unease. Why meet secretly when such meetings were considered taboo?

I considered different scenarios.

They wanted to discuss another council member.

Possibly.

They were planning a surprise party.

Highly unlikely.

Before I could think of a third, Nicole called.

"I think I found something interesting."

"Good. An agenda item?"

"Uh, huh. It appears there's a rezoning request for the Mirror Lake Inn."

I sat up.

"Has it been voted on?"

"I checked all the related information and found it curious that the vote is tied."

"Which means a swing vote is needed to pass the request. Excellent, Nicole."

"What do you think it means?"

"I have no idea."

"Try to dig further. I have to go. Ingrid's home."

"Ask her to watch Teddy and join us for tea in the lobby. I'll gather more information."

"Good idea. I'll ask."

Ingrid kicked off her shoes and plopped on the sofa.

"It's good to be home. How did your day go?"

She rested her feet on the coffee table.

"It's still going. I need a favor. Tell me if you're too tired and I'll understand."

"If you want me to watch Teddy, I'll be happy too. He's a delight."

I breathed a sigh of relief.

"Perfect. The ladies want to meet for tea at the inn. We think we may have something."

"Care to share with the class?"

"If you let me make you a cup of tea."

I stood and headed for the kitchen.

"Thanks, Jillian."

"Ingrid, have you heard any talk of rezoning the inn? Say from the city council?"

She shook her head.

"I've never heard anything."

I handed her a cup of tea.

"Thanks. You must have been talking to our city councilmen today."

"Bingo. It turns out Drew Olson met with the two of them the night Gumm was killed."

"At the inn?"

"Right next to the kitchen."

James served us delicious Earl Grey tea as we sat by the fire munching on chocolate chip cookies.

"I could get used to this." I took a sip from the porcelain cup.

"Ingrid didn't mind taking Teddy, I see." Nicole took out her phone.

"I made some notes you two may find interesting."

"We're all ears." Ann leaned in.

Nicole lowered her voice.

"According to the files, the inn has been a moderate source of revenue for the city. It's not the only one. Lake Placid has a plethora of resorts and hotels."

I looked at Ann.

"We're with you so far."

"However, it sits on a valuable piece of property."

"How valuable?" I asked.

"Valuable enough for foreign investors to show an interest in buying it."

"And if they did buy it, would anything change?" Ann eyed the cake stand holding the last cookie.

"Go on, Ann. It has your name on it."

She didn't need any further coaxing.

"I'll be right back. Wait for me."

James deftly offered us refills.

The inn held charm. If it were sold, would the charm disappear?

Ann returned with a fresh cookie on a napkin.

Nicole resumed her notes.

"I looked up backgrounds on two interested parties. One is from the Arab Emirates, the other one is from China."

"Why here?" I asked. "Why Lake Placid?"

"I've seen it happen before. Commercial real estate replaces residential and vice versa. Think urban redevelopment."

"How can the inn be redeveloped? I can see remodeled but...."

"No. I see what Nicole is referring to. If someone bought the inn, someone with lots of capitol, they could make it into whatever they wanted."

"High end condos for instance?" I said.

"Condos could bring in property taxes for the city. Perhaps more than hotel taxes on room rates." Nicole put her phone on the table and drank her tea.

"Great job on research, Nicole." Ann sighed. "Now we need to find if it ties in to a motive."

"Murder often ties in to money." I crossed my arms to think.

"I don't believe you're finished, Nicole."

She set her tea on the table.

"I'm not?"

"No. We need to find out about the Olson family's financial affairs. Drew Olson in particular."

"You want her to hack into their financial affairs, Jillian?"

I shrugged.

"We want to find out if there's a motive, don't we?"

Ann nodded.

"Okay. But we never had this conversation."

Nicole shrugged.

"What conversation?"

I smiled and finished my tea.

As far as Drew went, I would choose to believe he was innocent until proven guilty.

At this point, I gave him a fifty-fifty chance.

CHAPTER SIXTEEN

While Nicole was on her fact-finding mission, my spirit told me to have a talk with Chief Taylor. What I couldn't understand was why he closed the investigation.

"Care to join me in a visit with the chief, Ann?"

"Honestly, I will be more effective observing the staff."

"Good idea. Let's all meet for dinner and share what we discover."

She handed me the keys.

"Good luck with Chief Taylor."

Butterflies fluttered in my stomach.

Ingrid didn't mind watching Teddy for a few more minutes after I texted the reason.

I climbed into the SUV grabbing onto the support handle and hoisting myself up. It was a good thing I didn't have to do this in my car back home.

After I Googled directions to the station, I prayed Chief Taylor was in.

The station was a two-story brick building at the other end of Main Street. I remember passing it when we first came into town.

The office was quiet except for an officer working at the front desk.

I scanned the bulletin board. A lost dog poster of a Shih-Tzu caught my eye.

This was a small town.

The officer raised his head.

"Can I help you, ma'am."

Try not to cringe, Jillian. You do have a few wrinkles.

"I would like to speak with Chief Taylor on a personal matter, please."

"Just a moment." He pressed a button. "Someone here to see you, sir. Name, ma'am?"

"Bradley, Jillian Bradley."

The officer returned to the call.

"He'll see you. Second door on the left."

Thank goodness, he was in.

Chief Taylor met me at his door.

"Mrs. Bradley? Come in and have a seat. I'm taking a coffee break. Want a cup?"

"Thanks – black is fine."

"I'll be right back."

The chief returned with two mismatched mugs and handed me one.

He closed the door, sat behind his desk piled with paperwork, and took a sip of his coffee.

"How can I help you? Did you lose your dog?"

"Teddy's at Ingrid's. I noticed the lost dog poster in front. Cases like that must keep you busy."

"If you're referring to my fishing the other day...."

"I apologize, Chief. The remark was cynical and uncalled for."

"No problem. We do work on cases, whether you think so or not. They're not always on display for the public, however."

"What about the murder of George Gumm? Ingrid said you closed the case. I'd like to know if you have a suspect."

"You're a feisty one, aren't you, Mrs. Bradley. I will tell you I have a suspect, but don't ask me who."

"Okay. I appreciate the need for confidentiality. But hear me."

"I'm listening."

"The police often solve cases with only one clue. A clue which can come from ordinary citizens like my friends and me."

"Do you think a couple of strangers know more than we do?"

"Perhaps you don't *know* what you know. I'm sounding mysterious but I have had experience."

"Why don't you tell me what I know, Mrs. Bradley and I'll tell you whether it pertains to the investigation or not – sound fair?"

"Sounds fair. Please understand my intentions are to help, not get in the way."

He nodded.

"As long as you don't get in the way."

I studied him. Was he threatening me?

I sipped my coffee.

"Here's what I believe you know, Chief. No one liked Gumm. Even though Eva loved him, she only tolerated him. Gumm sexually harassed Claire Hunt causing her husband to confront him on the night on the night he was murdered."

"I wasn't aware of the harassment. Go on. You're doing fine."

"Gumm hit Sam, went back inside the kitchen, and the altercation was witnessed by Will Pratt."

"Anything else?"

"Were you aware that Quincy Monroe thought Gumm got what he deserved? Or he had animosity toward the chef because he stifled his pay?"

"What do you mean by stifled his pay?"

"I'll set that aside for a moment. I'm not finished."

He shifted in his chair.

"Did Sam tell you he heard a noise in the parking lot after Will Pratt drove by? Or that Gumm yelled at someone leaving the kitchen by the back door before the altercation?"

The chief sat quietly, put his hands together, and crossed his legs.

"You've withheld information."

"Oh, no I haven't. I'm giving it to you now."

"Truce?"

"The choice is yours." I sipped my coffee and waited to hear what he had to say.

"You have my formal apology, ma'am."

"I'll accept but only if you stop calling me ma'am or Mrs. Bradley. They make me feel old."

"Okay, Jillian. I'll try. Your information might be helpful. I'd like to talk to Quincy Morgan and get his alibi."

"Good."

"Is there anything else you've learned that I may know?"

He smiled.

"My friends and I are working on it. Let's say I have a hunch."

"It's interesting you use that terminology."

"Why is that?"

"I have a hunch, too."

I thanked him for seeing me, and felt strides were made in getting his cooperation. It would be interesting too if our investigations dovetailed.

The meeting left me tired and hungry. I needed to get home to Teddy and make his supper.

At least there was time for play before meeting Ann and Nicole.

He ran to greet me, tail wagging as I came through the door.

"Woof! Woof!" he barked.

"So I get a two bark greeting this afternoon."

After setting my purse down, I picked him up and gave him some love.

"Cup of tea, Jillian?" Ingrid came from the kitchen drying her hands.

"No thanks. I've just had coffee with Chief Taylor."

I sniffed cinnamon in the air. "Something smells good."

"I'm baking an apple pie. It seemed appropriate for a fall day."

I thought of Chief Taylor and Drew being single. Did they ever get such a treat? I didn't know any men who baked, but I suppose there were some.

"Do you have vanilla ice cream?"

She snapped her fingers.

"I knew there was something I forgot."

"I'll stop by after dinner and pick some up."

"Bring Ann and Nicole back with you and we'll have pie and coffee."

"You've made an offer we can't refuse!"

Teddy waited patiently with his favorite toy I'd brought, a blue stuffed pig, clutched in his mouth.

I grabbed it away and threw it across the room.

"Fetch!" I said.

He ran as fast as his little legs would carry him, grabbed the pig in his teeth, and raced back.

I wrestled it playfully away before throwing it again.

After four tugs of war, it was finally time for his dinner.

Ingrid lifted the apple pie from the oven and set it on a trivet on the counter.

"Tell me about Chief Taylor. Did you make any progress?"

I took a poached chicken breast from the refrigerator and chopped it into small bites for Teddy.

"He said he'd talk to Quincy Morgan and get his alibi. It's something."

"That name sounds familiar. Sam may have mentioned him."

"He may have. We paid a visit to Hunt's Produce Farm and chatted with him. Quincy made a statement to the effect he'd replaced Sam."

"I hardly think that's true. According to Claire, Sam belongs in farming. Like most young men

Sam has the need to find his own direction in life."

"Even if the direction leads back home."

She nodded and smiled.

"He's a good boy. Loves Claire. Jillian, we simply must find a way to clear him of Gumm's murder. We must!"

Tears sprang from her eyes catching me off guard.

I patted her shoulder.

"Now stop worrying. Your friends won't let you down. We won't quit until the truth is uncovered."

She sniffed and grabbed a tissue off the counter.

"I'm sorry. The stress is getting me down. Claire, too."

"It's going to be okay. And you know what? Even if Sam was guilty, and I don't believe he is, you and Claire will get through it."

"This situation reminds me of when my husband died. What a nightmare it was."

"But you survived and you will also get through this."

"Thanks, Jillian. You're right. Look at you – you've lost two husbands and still you take time to help people like me."

"It's my nature. I can't stand injustice."

I put water out for Teddy and glanced at the time.

Ingrid covered the warm apple pie with foil.

"Changing the subject, where are you girls going for dinner?"

"We're open for suggestions."

"You may want to try Caffe Rustica. I like their cioppino."

"Oh, seafood sounds good. Thanks."

"They have an interesting menu. I'll give them that."

"Now I'm curious."

Our dinner was excellent. We shared a savory appetizer of antipasti, almost a meal in itself, and ordered bowls of cioppino, a wonderful fish stew in a mildly spicy tomato broth served with garlic crostini – small baguette slices spread with olive oil, sprinkled with salt and pepper, baked until golden brown then rubbed with fresh garlic.

Nicole and Ann gave kudos all around.

"Nicole, did you find anything online this afternoon?" I asked halfway through our meal.

"I did, but we'd better wait until we get to Ingrid's before I tell you. Too many ears."

"I agree. Let me Google the closest grocery store and we'll get some ice cream." I whipped out my iPhone as we piled into the SUV and headed to Ingrid's.

"There's one up ahead." Ann nodded toward the right.

"Would you both like to come in with me?"

"Sure." Nicole patted her tummy. "I need the exercise after that meal."

"Me, too." Ann parked in front of the store.

At the back of the market in the refrigeration section, I caught a familiar profile studying the frozen desserts.

I stepped toward the figure of Chief Taylor.

"We couldn't interest you in a slice of freshly baked apple pie and ice cream, could we?"

I selected the best brand of vanilla I could find.

He studied the carton as Ann and Nicole joined us.

"Hi, Chief," Ann said.

"Hello, Chief Taylor." Nicole smiled.

"It's not often I get an invitation from three lovely ladies like this. I'll be happy to join you."

On the way out, he followed us to the checkout counter.

"Good," I said. "Meet us at Ingrid's. I'm sure she'd love to have you."

"I hope I won't be intruding."

"Trust us, Chief," Nicole said. "You won't be."

"Why don't you go ahead of us since we only have ice cream?"

"Thanks."

He checked what few items were in his basket and paid the cashier.

"I'll be over after I put away the groceries."

"Don't be too long." I shook a finger.

"With apple pie and ice cream waiting? Don't worry."

On the way home, Ann said to me, "He seems friendlier."

"We declared a truce this afternoon. And why shouldn't we? We both want justice for Eva."

"Don't you think you should let Ingrid know he's coming?" Nicole was always the considerate one.

"I'll send a text. She invited you both so it shouldn't be a problem."

Chief Taylor showed up at Ingrid's shortly after we arrived.

Apple pie and coffee were waiting.

Teddy sat happily in my lap as we enjoyed the scrumptious cinnamon laced dessert, making oohs and ahs over the tender flaky crust. He politely took the small bites I gave him.

After Ingrid refilled our coffee, Chief Taylor sat back in the overstuffed chair and smiled.

"Ingrid, the pie was delicious. A real treat for a single man like myself."

She beamed.

"Thanks for coming over to share it. We do appreciate whatever you're doing to get to the bottom of Chef Gumm's murder."

"I know, believe me. After Jillian stopped in this afternoon, I went to talk to Quincy Morgan."

"Quincy?" Ingrid seemed surprised. "He works for Sam's dad, doesn't he?"

The chief nodded.

"He seemed almost cocky by the way he acted when I asked his whereabouts that night."

"Did he have an alibi?" I ate the last delicious bite of ice cream.

"It had holes. No one can vouch for him. I thought he was evasive."

Teddy yipped, jumped from my lap, and ran to the front door.

Chief Taylor set his plate down, and rose, and went to investigate.

Fritz bounded in wagging his tail. Eva was behind him.

"Eva! Come in."

"Hello, Mark. I'm so sorry."

She looked down as if embarrassed.

"Fritz got out when I took out the trash and ran over here. He must have wanted company."

Ingrid ushered Eva into the living room.

"Hello, Jillian. Ladies."

Ingrid chuckled. "Fritz must have smelled my apple pie. There's one piece left. Would you like some?"

"I'd appreciate it if you'd take the temptation from me," Chief Taylor said.

She smiled and seemed to blush.

"Why don't we split it?"

"I'll be right back," Ingrid said.

Eva sat on the sofa next to me.

Chief Taylor couldn't take his eyes off her.

He rubbed Fritz's ears.

"I'm glad Fritz escaped," I said.

"It gets lonely, especially at night," Eva said.

Ingrid returned with fresh plates of pie and ice cream.

Eva glanced around the room.

"So is this a meeting of some kind?" she asked.

"You could say that," I said.

"Eva, what do you know about your husband's relationship with Quincy Morgan?"

She put down her fork.

CHAPTER SEVENTEEN

"Mark, did Quincy kill Gumby?" Eva asked.

"We still don't know. Did he and George ever argue?"

Eva's chin quivered.

"I'm sorry. It's difficult trying to talk about it."

"We understand," I said. "But if you can shed any light on this man, we may be able to help you find closure."

"Okay. You may be right."

Ingrid rose.

"I'll get more coffee."

After a deep breath, Eva spoke. "I do remember a recent afternoon. Gumby came home for a break and was angry about something."

Ingrid refilled Eva's cup.

"He complained about the prices of inferior produce. He mentioned Quincy's name."

"What did he say?" I urged.

"It was curious. It was almost as if he was accusing Quincy of cheating him. I didn't understand at first because Gumby was yelling."

"Did he get this way often?" Ann asked.

Eva shook her head.

"My husband's job took all of his time. He was a workaholic leaving nothing for us."

"So you're saying he vented his stress at home...with you." Nicole seemed to understand.

Eva nodded.

"No one understands how difficult it was juggling three restaurants at once. I suppose an inferior and overpriced supplier was Gumby's breaking point."

I turned to Chief Taylor.

"Sam said he heard a noise near the dumpster after Gumm hit him."

Ingrid sat on sofa listening intently.

I searched my brain.

"What did he say before that? Now I remember!"

Chief Taylor leaned in.

"You've had your last chance. Yes, that's what Sam thought he heard Gumm yell. And then he slammed the door."

"It fits." Eva seemed thoughtful.

"Gumby was going to change vendors." He mumbled as he played with Fritz so he was barely audible.

Ingrid collected our empty dishes.

"I hope this doesn't mean you think Quincy stabbed him. He's a friend of the family – devoted to Sam's dad."

I moved to help.

Chief Taylor carried his plate to the kitchen and returned to the living room.

"I'll see Eva home. Come on, Fritz." Fritz obeyed, wagging his tail.

Teddy followed them to the door.

"Thanks for the great pie, Ingrid." The chief extended his hand.

"Anytime, Chief."

"Goodnight, ladies. We'll talk soon."

Eva nodded to us, attached a leash to Fritz, and preceded Chief Taylor out the door.

"We should be getting back, too." Ann took keys from her purse. "Ready, Nicole?"

"Whenever you are."

Ann gave Ingrid a peck on the cheek.

"The pie was a treat. Thank you for having us."

"Thanks for the ice cream."

A worried look crossed Ingrid's face.

After my friends left, I patted her back.

"We're making progress, don't you think?" I asked.

"I only hope Sam is telling the truth about what he heard."

"Why would he lie?"

"I'm afraid to speculate."

I did not understand.

"Do you think Sam was making up a story to shift blame?"

"I think Sam would say anything to keep from losing Claire. I'm tired – it's been a long evening. And I still need to wash up."

"You go to bed and let me stick these dishes in the dishwasher. I insist. Besides, the pie was worth it."

She smiled.

"Thanks, Jillian. And thanks for all you and your friends are doing to help Sam. I want so badly to believe he's innocent."

"Me, too. Now off to bed."

As I rinsed the dishes and put them into the dishwasher, I thought about Quincy's relationship to the Hunts.

Ingrid said he was a friend of the family.

How well was Gumm's harassment of Claire known?

Did Quincy know?

He said he'd taken Sam's place at the farm.

Would he have lost his job if Gumm was unhappy with his deliveries?

Something occurred to me.

What if Quincy delivered inferior produce to the inn, and sold the better food elsewhere?

I shrugged.

Who would know?

It was time for us to do some investigating.

I texted Ann asking her to pick me up for breakfast in the morning.

Teddy sprawled on the kitchen floor close to his water bowl.

"A little doggie needs to go to bed."

When I spoke, he raised his head.

"Let me wipe off the counter first and I'll carry you to the room."

He gave a muffled woof.

Before turning off the lights in the living room, I glanced out the front window.

Chief Taylor and Eva sat on her porch.

What if they're in a relationship? They seem terribly close.

With Teddy in my arms, I walked to the room, closed the door, and readied for bed.

As I lay in the darkness, my unbridled thoughts turned to Vincent.

Did he find someone else?

Would I ever know?

A tear escaped from my eye.

Stop it. Vincent is still your friend.

If I believed he was, why the nagging doubts? Men.

Dogs may be easier.

Drew Olson popped into my mind displacing thoughts of Vincent.

I liked Eva's brother. He was a great cook, interesting, and amusing. Having gardening for a hobby was also a plus.

It would be interesting to find out from Nicole the family's financial dynamics.

After pounding my pillow into a comfortable position, I closed my eyes and turned off my brain.

Goodnight, Lord.

The Bluesberry Bakery was a pet friendly storefront on Main Street serving scrumptious scones, Linzer tarts, strudels, and delicious coffee. From the name, I wondered if the owners were jazz lovers with a name like "Bluesberry."

Choosing what to order was a difficult decision. The pastries all looked so good. I finally settled on a blueberry scone and a cappuccino.

Ann tried the strudel and Nicole chose a Linzer tart.

We found a table and chairs outside, and settled in for breakfast.

Teddy sat at attention by my feet, with his warm brown eyes on my scone.

After spreading a piece with butter and jam, I tossed him a bite.

"What have you found out, Nicole?" I asked.

"A few things I believe you'll find interesting."

Ann and I leaned in.

"Since Drew's mother passed away, he and Eva own equal shares of the inn. She's solvent – he is not."

I raised my eyebrows.

"Too many ex-wives to support, probably." I was disappointed at the news.

"Not only does he pay alimony, his credit cards are at their limit. Despite what he may have led us to believe, Drew Olson travels extensively."

"And here I thought he was tied to the inn with little time off." I didn't like being deceived.

"There's more." Nicole took a bite of her tart. "This is wonderful!"

After swallowing, she continued.

"It appears one of the foreign investors has made a recent bid to buy the inn for a hefty sum."

Ann sat back and sipped her coffee.

"Did you find any information on whether or not the council has voted on the zoning change?"

Nicole glanced around then back to Ann and me.

"The council met after Gumm was murdered. The vote passed."

"Drew is going to sell the inn?" I was flabbergasted. "Eva never said a word."

Nicole shook her head.

"Maybe she doesn't know."

A delivery truck marked "Hunt's Produce Farm" on the side barreled down the street.

Quincy Morgan waved to us as he passed.

"Ladies," I said. "I'm not satisfied we know the whole story between Quincy and Sam Hunt."

"Maybe we should pay Sam a visit." Ann finished her strudel and wiped the corner of her mouth with a small paper napkin.

"Or Claire." Nicole offered.

"Why not talk to them both?" I asked. "They may be home – it's still early. I can take us to their apartment."

"I'm ready." Nicole gathered our trash and stuck it in the trashcan.

"Let's go." Ann smiled. "Don't forget Teddy."

I bent down, gathered him in my arms, and we all headed for the SUV.

We passed several galleries I wished to explore.

"Maybe later we'll have time for some shopping."

"Let's plan on it." Ann found the complex where Sam and Claire lived and turned in.

A definite chill blew through the air as we stepped from the SUV.

I again admired the views of dense forests bursting with blazes of color set against the blue Adirondacks. The gorgeous fall displays make our trip worthwhile.

We trudged up the three flights of stairs until we arrived at apartment 374, completely worn out. Apartments were definitely for young people.

I knocked gently.

Sam immediately opened the door and stepped back.

"Mrs. Bradley!"

Claire stood behind him.

"Well, let them in, Sam."

The aroma of bacon frying suggested they were having breakfast.

"Sure. Don't mind me. I'm just surprised to see you this early."

"And we apologize. You remember Ann and Nicole?"

He nodded.

"Yeah, from The Cottage."

He pulled out chairs for us to sit.

"Don't worry – I can stand and eat my breakfast. Do it all the time."

"Thank you. We won't stay long, I promise." I held Teddy close.

"How about some coffee? I can make another pot."

Ann shook her hand.

"We've had ours, thanks."

"Why did you come?" Claire asked. "It's not bad news, is it?"

I shook my head.

"No. We only want you to tell us about Quincy Morgan."

Sam shrugged.

"Dad hired him to help at the farm when I went away to school. Dad liked to help troubled kids."

Claire couldn't take her eyes off Teddy.

"May I hold him?"

I handed him to her.

"I really want a dog like this. Sam says he'll buy me one as soon as he can afford it." She cast him a loving glance.

"One of these days." He inhaled his bacon and eggs and started in on a slice of toast. "Claire also has things she wants to do first."

"True. I think working on a cruise ship would be a great way to travel and see the world, don't you, Mrs. Bradley?"

"As long as you don't get seasick." Nicole was right.

"Of course it would leave mom alone." Claire stared into her coffee.

Ann shifted in her chair and crossed her arms. "Sam, what did you mean about troubled kids? Was Quincy ever in trouble?"

"He came close to getting arrested once for shoplifting in high school but there wasn't enough proof. His mom put him in the school for boys after it happened."

"And after that?" I asked.

"Quincy didn't ever cause trouble after he was put in that school. They watch you like a hawk."

"What about after he went to work for your dad?"

Sam shrugged.

"I left, so I wouldn't know. Sometimes we hang out together at the bowling alley. He's always telling me how lucky I am to have Claire."

"How is he with Claire?"

"What do you mean?"

"Does he ever flirt with her, or seem protective of her?"

The couple looked at each other.

"Quincy has always been nice to me." Claire seemed worried. "Why are you asking these questions?"

"Claire, I must ask you if he knew about the harassment at work."

I waited.

"I don't think he ever witnessed it."

"But you're not sure?" Ann asked.

Sam spoke.

"Quincy and I had a conversation about it once – it may have been at the bowling alley."

"When was this?" Nicole asked. "It may be important."

"The last time we all went bowling was the weekend before Gumm was killed. That rat harassed Claire twice before I confronted him."

Claire grew wide-eyed.

"Sam. You did say something, I remember."

"How did Quincy react?" I asked.

Sam looked at his wife.

"He didn't say a word."

CHAPTER EIGHTEEN

Our conversation with Sam and Claire had me worried. If there was a possibility Quincy Morgan was the killer, it meant someone unhinged was loose on the public.

As I listened to church bells in the distance, I was reminded that God was still in control.

Lord, please protect my friends and me. And Teddy, too.

There had been instances in the past when my little companion faced danger because of my sleuthing – I didn't want it to happen again.

Ann, Nicole, and I realized we needed to go shopping – therapy for clearing our minds, as we regarded possible facts in the murder.

"Ann, up ahead on the left is a gallery I'd like to visit."

"I see it." She found a spot and parked.

With Teddy safely inside his tote, the three of us perused the Cornerstone Rustic & Craft Gallery.

The shop was filled with beautiful hand crafted ceramics, wood and metal sculptures, and other works of art.

"This is a stunning necklace." I held up a hand blown Murano glass beaded strand in colors of amber, blue, and rose. I was in love.

Nicole smiled. "It's lovely."

"You could wear it home and not have to pack it." Ann was always so practical.

"I'll buy it. And look over here." I led the girls to a section of gift baskets. "Look at this one for gardeners."

"Are you thinking of giving it to Ingrid?" Nicole asked.

"It's perfect for her." Ann ran her hand over the rustic weave.

"It would make a nice hostess gift. I'll get it, too."

Nicole found a blue and purple silk scarf she couldn't pass up. She wrapped it around her neck.

"What do you think?"

"It's you, Nicole." Ann nodded and wandered over to the hand blown glass area.

She selected a teal and silver vase. "These are my colors. I'm buying it for my collection."

The glass souvenir was perfect. It would fit into the decor of her lovely home. Hopefully, the beautiful colors would remind her of the fun part of our trip.

"You'll have to have it shipped home, don't you think?" Nicole asked.

"No, it's only 5" tall. I can carry it on the plane."

Purchases in hand, we moved to the next item of business. Lunch.

"Do we walk and scout for a place or drive?" Ann asked.

"We're limited with Teddy." I searched up and down the street. Nothing looked appealing.

"Would you ladies mind eating at The Cottage again? They will let Teddy join us outside."

"Their menu is delicious and varied," Nicole replied.

"The Cottage it is." Ann led the way to the SUV.

The place was crowded. After waiting ten minutes, the host seated us outside.

"Look at this view." Ann said. "Breathtaking!"

We sat at the edge of Mirror Lake and dined under an umbrella. Ducks swam past, a canoer rowed by, and a gentle breeze stirred the air.

This was a lovely place. Who wouldn't want to live in a condo here?

"If Drew Olson and Eva were to sell, I think it would be a shame to lose the inn. It's such a landmark, almost a symbol of Lake Placid." I studied the menu.

"True," Ann said as she closed her menu and gave her order. "I'm going to have the chicken apricot sandwich."

"I'm going to order the short rib tacos. They sound different." Nicole was being adventurous today. "What are you having, Jillian?"

"The shrimp `a la Cottage looks interesting. I'll try that. Besides, Teddy will like the cheese."

He poked up his head at the mention of the word and pricked up his ears.

"Be a good dog and I'll give you a bite."

He wagged his tail in anticipation.

Ann seemed startled.

"Jillian. Drew Olson just came in." Ann waved.

"Why are you waving?" I asked.

"Just as I thought." She smiled. "He's heading this way."

Nicole sipped her water. "Probably to see you, Jillian."

I turned red.

Drew smiled at us on his way to our table.

"Nice to see all of you." He beamed. "Thanks for choosing The Cottage to have lunch."

"Would you care to join us?" I asked. What else could I say?

He pulled out the fourth chair.

"Thanks, I'd love to."

"How are things going at the inn?" Nicole asked.

The server brought our food and took Drew's order.

Drew waited to answer until he left.

"Not that great. Chef Gumm's death has reflected in the number of reservations and guests are leaving early. Nothing like a murder to frighten off vacationers."

"I'm so sorry," I said. "Will you be able to recover?"

He shrugged.

"Time will tell. As general manager, my duties are turning me gray."

I studied his head. There were a few strands of gray but not many.

"You're probably overreacting. Have you ever considered selling?"

He leaned into the table.

"I'd sell in a minute."

"I thought the inn was a family legacy," Ann said.

He paused then looked at her.

"Legacy? For whom? Me? I don't care about being shackled until I'm too old to enjoy life."

Nicole crossed her arms and cocked her head.

"What does Eva say? As your sister, isn't she part owner?"

"Eva? I don't think she really cares. When her husband was alive, it meant him having a job. Now? I don't know."

"Maybe you should talk to her." I said. "Sometimes a fresh start can be a good thing. Especially when you lose someone."

"Perhaps I will."

His cell phone buzzed.

"Excuse me, ladies. I need to take this call. Thanks for letting me join you."

"Our pleasure." Ann hid a smile.

What Drew shared was honest and open. Short of mentioning the secret meeting with the other two city council members, he seemed an unlikely killer.

"Well ladies. I'm ready to leave whenever you are. Teddy needs a walk."

We paid our checks and returned to the SUV.

"I'll drop you off if you like, Jillian." Ann started the engine.

"I'll walk from the parking lot. It will help me work off lunch."

"Stay in touch," Nicole said. "I think I'm going to take a nap."

"Sounds good to me, too." Ann drove a short distance to across the street and parked behind the inn.

"See you ladies, later."

I attached Teddy's leash and set him on the ground.

"Woof!" he barked.

Even though I tried steering him along the side of the road, he kept pulling to the right, determined to lead me to something.

I followed him to the dumpster.

Great. Teddy was leading me to the trash. I'm sure there were great things for him to smell.

"Whoa, Teddy. Where are you going?"

He squeezed in behind the large garbage receptacle and yipped.

I pulled him back and took a look. Using my phone's light I scanned the area.

There it was. A single piece of trash wadded up and stuck under the bin.

Teddy was wild – definitely excited at what he'd found.

"Teddy, why are you acting like this? It's only a piece of trash. Bad dog!"

He was unwavering.

I reached down and carefully plucked the piece from the ground.

Teddy wanted to sniff it so badly that he pawed my legs trying to reach his discovery.

I unraveled what appeared to be a receipt marked with items circled in red and punctuated with explanation points.

"Oh, my. This is an invoice for Hunt's Produce Farm. Teddy, look at the date – it's the same day Chef Gumm was murdered."

Teddy whined then let out a loud "woof" as if to say, "I told you I found something important."

"We need to have Chief Taylor take a look at this. It may have fingerprints and I'll give you one guess whose they might be."

I called the chief immediately.

After we reached Ingrid's, I took the invoice, handling it as little as possible, found a zip-lock bag, and placed it inside.

Chief Taylor arrived shortly afterward and I let him in.

"Thanks for coming, Chief. What Teddy found may not be important but I didn't want to overlook a possible clue."

"You did the right thing, Jillian. May I see it?"

I handed him the plastic bag.

"Thanks for protecting the evidence."

I shrugged.

"Force of habit, I suppose."

"So this is an invoice from Hunt's Produce Farm."

"Dated the day of the murder."

"So you think Quincy was the noise Sam heard behind the dumpster that night."

"It fits. What if Quincy took that receipt from Gumm's kitchen to cover his being there?"

"If he did, why didn't it make it *into* the dumpster instead of under it?"

"Good question. Chief, let's replay that night."

"Mind if I sit?"

"No, I'm sorry – sit anywhere you like."

"Okay – replay away."

"Sam said he heard Chef Gumm yell at someone – someone in the parking lot who may have just left the kitchen."

"I'm with you so far."

"Sam goes into the kitchen and has it out with him over Claire. Gumm throws him out, they argue in the parking lot, and Gumm strikes him."

"I'm with you so far – it's entirely possible."

"Good. Sam hears a noise behind the dumpster. Was it Quincy? If so, maybe he hid to watch when the two came out of the kitchen and didn't have a chance to dispose of the invoice."

"If that's true, why is it all crumpled?"

"I believe Quincy was angry. Angry at the way Gumm treated Sam. Or angry at Gumm' notes on the invoice. He could have wadded it up without even realizing he was doing it."

"I'm with you so far. Of course, this is all speculation, Jillian."

"I know – but when Teddy alerts me to something, it usually turns out to be a clue."

Chief Taylor gave a look of doubt.

"I don't care what you think, Chief. I know Teddy's capabilities."

"Fine. Let's say Quincy did as you speculate. Why then didn't he let Sam know he was watching and help him up?"

"Good question. The answer lies in what Quincy did next. It wasn't to help Sam, we know that."

"We also know Quincy hasn't been forthcoming about where he was that night. But all we have is circumstantial evidence."

"True. But there's something else."

The chief looked alert.

"Someone followed me to Sam's apartment a few days ago, I'm almost positive. It may have been Quincy keeping an eye on me."

The chief smiled.

"I have a confession."

Now it was my turned to be surprised.

"What?"

"I might as well let you in on something. The person following you was one of my men."

"Why were you having me tailed?"

"Because I thought you needed protection. Really – it was my only motivation."

"I see. I thought...."

"You thought the killer may have been following you?"

I nodded.

"I'm relieved in a way. Why did you think I needed protecting? You should tell me what you know if you think you can trust me."

"I think I can trust you – you're far too pure hearted."

"I'm a believer, if that's what you mean."

"Right. I am, too. So is Eva. Tell you what. Let's make a deal and cooperate with each other.

You've proven to me with your call that we both want the same thing."

"Justice."

"Deal?"

"Deal."

"Here's why I think you need protection."

CHAPTER NINETEEN

After Chief Taylor explained the situation regarding the death of Drew and Eva's mother, I was shaken.

Her death sounded suspicious from the beginning. Now I was sure. It was no accident.

Chief Taylor's challenge was to determine the reason for her death and the perpetrator.

The autopsy revealed Mrs. Olson died of asphyxiation, which meant someone smothered her before throwing her body out onto the pavement.

Horrible! And criminal.

I shuddered picturing this happening to my own mother who was approximately the same age.

The killer needed to be stopped.

The chief stood, ready to leave.

"I must get back to the station, but I'll check on Eva first."

"You care about her, don't you?"

Teddy marched into the room from the kitchen, water dripping from the fur around his mouth.

"It's time for his nap." I scooped him up.

"You care about Teddy, don't you?"

"I get your point. I'm being a busybody, aren't I?"

"Eva and I have been friends since high school. You're right. I do care about her. She's vulnerable."

Was he inferring something about Drew? It was difficult to tell. Maybe now that we had a deal, he would be more forthcoming than he was before.

With a tip of his brow, Chief Taylor walked out the door and made his way to Eva's, next door.

I sighed.

"Be careful, my friend. This isn't over yet."

After my day of shopping and investigating, I needed a nap.

I took the new necklace from the sack and admired the workmanship.

One of a kind.

Chef Gumm had also been one of a kind. Just the wrong kind.

Chief Taylor was right. Circumstantial evidence was not enough to put Quincy at the scene of the crime.

Sam was there, too.

How could we get Quincy to tell us what happened between him and Gumm?

As I lay on the bed resting, I tried to put myself in Quincy's place. If I were he, what would I want?

A better contract for more pay? He had said as much.

To be Sam and Claire's friend? He had hung out with them at the bowling alley.

To protect Claire? He knew about the harassment.

To gain respect? He seemed proud when he mentioned taking Sam's place on the Hunt farm. Being yelled at would be demeaning.

Or maybe the reason was still hidden.

I was sleepy.

Teddy was sleeping soundly.

Soon I was, too.

My eyes popped open.

"What if...?"

A text from Ann came in on my phone:

Need to meet in our room ASAP – we have news.

So much for the nap.

Teddy popped up his head at my movement and looked at me as if to say, "Any trouble, mistress?"

"Go back to sleep, little one."

"Woof!"

He must have heard Ingrid coming home.

After slipping on my shoes, I re-combed my hair and went into the living room to talk to Ingrid.

"I'm so glad you're home."

"You and me both. What's the matter? You look worried, Jillian."

"Ann has a piece of news – she didn't say what, only wants to talk as soon as possible."

"Go on then, I'll watch Teddy for you and get his supper."

"You're an angel, Ingrid. Thank you. By the way, I have a gift for you – it's in the kitchen."

"A gift?"

She raced into the kitchen and brought out the gift basket I'd bought.

"So many goodies – I love the basket."

"I think it's for cut flowers. I'm glad you like it. You've been a lifesaver watching Teddy for me."

"He's been a delight. Now you go on and meet your friends. Don't worry about Teddy – we'll be fine."

"Thanks, Ingrid. I'll call if I'm going to be late."

After a brisk walk to the inn, I took the elevator to their room. The door was ajar for me to enter as soon as I arrived.

"Ladies?" I said.

"Jillian. Have a seat." Ann motioned to the wingback chair.

"What's all the excitement?"

Nicole secured the door. "Before we went downstairs for tea a few minutes ago, I was looking for a brochure of the inn to take home."

"They were on a table in front of the reception desk." Ann picked up the story.

"John Peterson was working the afternoon shift. When he saw us, he looked around and seemed like he wanted to talk."

"Go on."

"He said he had information about the night of the murder we might be interested in." Nicole said.

Ann began to pace.

"Bottom line is – Drew Olson brought the key from the walk-in freezer and put it in its usual place. John showed us."

"What time was this? Did he say?"

"It was late, around 10:30 or 11:00 p.m. It was curious because John told us Chef Gumm was in charge of the key."

It made sense. The one in charge of the kitchen made sure the freezer was secure of theft.

Something Drew said when we talked on the night he made dinner nagged at my brain.

"You ladies have done a good job. This puts Drew at the scene of the crime at the time of the murder. Not good concerning his alibi."

I needed to talk to Drew. We never discussed what *he* was doing that night. Would he share with me? If not, he might have something to hide.

"If Drew is the killer, John Peterson may be in danger since he can testify he saw him at the time it happened.

"I'm calling Chief Taylor and letting him know what we've learned.'

Ann and Nicole heartily agreed.

Nicole put her hand on my arm.

"You like Drew, don't you."

"Yes, I do. And I think he likes me too. I'm going to talk to him and see if he'll tell me what really happened."

"Jillian, it could be dangerous," Ann said.

"Don't worry. I know what to do. You two enjoy dinner without me tonight. If anything happens, I'll let you know."

The investigation seemed to be ending. And yet after talking to Ann and Nicole there were more questions than answers.

I reflected on the clues as I walked to Ingrid's.

Were there any other possibilities someone else could have killed Gumm? It seemed Quincy had the strongest motive. And with finding the invoice dated the day of the murder, there was opportunity.

Drew could now be placed at the scene with John Peterson's testimony. As for the murder weapon, either could have wiped fingerprints clean.

If Drew murdered Gumm, there must be motive. Would he tell me? Perhaps my plan would allow him to do so without fear of recrimination.

Sam Hunt was Chief Taylor's prime suspect – of this, I had no doubt. He was seen by Chef Pratt in the parking lot as the last known person to see Gumm alive.

Sam had means, motive, and opportunity.

The chief had every right to believe he was guilty.

Was I partial in my feelings because of my friendship with Ingrid? Or because Claire was so sweet and innocent and didn't deserve to have her husband go to prison?

Halfway home I stopped by the boathouse and walked out on the pier. The Adirondack chairs were empty.

It was time to pray.

Father, please show me the truth. You know I like Drew, but don't let it cloud my thinking.

There's a protective spirit I have for Sam because of his family, but it's more important for justice to be served if he's guilty.

As for Quincy, he seems a tragic figure – troubled in his youth, living close to poverty, and treated badly by his client. Is he a victim of circumstance?

Which one, Lord? Which one?
It was time to execute my plan.

Teddy greeted me at Ingrid's front door. His little tail wagged so fast I thought it might fall off.

"Hello, sweet doggie. I missed you!" A kiss on top of his head and a gentle squeeze seemed to make him happy.

Ingrid came from the kitchen drying her hands on a towel.

"You're back early. Have you had dinner? Teddy scarfed his."

"I'm not hungry. A cup of tea would be nice."

"I'll make us some."

I followed her into the kitchen, holding Teddy, and sat at the table.

"This investigation has me a little worried."

"Why, has anything happened?"

I sighed.

"You might say it has. Ingrid, have you ever worked the inn's night shift?"

She nodded.

"When I first started, I did. What would you like to know?"

"Was Chef Gumm the last one to leave the kitchen at night?"

She thought a moment.

"Yes. Why?"

"I need to know what keys are left at the front desk at night."

"Let me think. As I recall only three people have keys to the kitchen. The general manager, Mr. Olson, the executive chef, and the executive sous chef. Those keys remain with them."

"And what about the keys to the walk in freezer?"

"Hmmm. Only the executive chef carries those. He leaves one at night at the front desk signifying the kitchen is closed."

"And the other one?"

"He keeps it."

Another piece of the puzzle fell into place.

"Thanks, Ingrid."

I finished my tea and glanced at the time.

"I'm meeting with Drew Olson in a few minutes. We're having dinner together."

"Really?"

She smiled as if amused.

"Don't get any ideas. I only want to talk to him. Besides, he's too much of a playboy for me."

"If you say so, Jillian. Take my car if you wish. I won't need it tonight. Want me to watch Teddy?"

"If you don't mind. Thank you."

"I'll get the keys."

"I'll only be a moment. I need to make a quick change and touch up a bit."

When I returned, Ingrid handed me the keys.

"Your dress is a stunner! Royal blue suits you."

"Thanks. Let's hope Drew thinks so, too."

"Good hunting," she said. "Teddy, do you want to play fetch?"

He pricked up his ears and followed her to the kitchen.

Ingrid found Teddy's favorite toy, the blue stuffed pig.

"Fetch!" She threw it across the room.

Teddy raced toward the prize.

Taking the opportunity for distraction, I slipped away.

Drew wanted sushi tonight. He suggested Aki on Main Street. Even though raw fish wasn't one of my favorites I agreed to meet him at six o'clock.

Aki was an intimate boutique restaurant on Main Street. A sandwich board by the front door displayed sushi specials for the day.

Drew was waiting for me inside.

"You look lovely."

He seemed sincere.

"Thank you. Did you get a table?"

"Ah, yes."

He signaled to the host who led us to a quiet table.

After pulling out my chair and helping me get settled, we studied the menus.

"Shall we order rolls to share or would you prefer your own entrées?" he asked, eyes glued to the menu.

"Why don't you order whatever you like? This is my treat."

A look of confusion crossed his face.

"If you insist. Thank you."

I searched for chicken teriyaki – a good old standby whenever Japanese was the fare of choice.

The server took our orders, filled our glasses with water, and returned with a pot of steeping hot tea. Smiling, he poured it into tiny cups.

I knew better but asked for sugar anyway.

We made small talk until the food arrived. I didn't want to frighten him by immediately plunging into his alibi.

"Your order looks like art." I always thought sushi should be admired instead of eaten.

"Why don't you care for it, Jillian?"

"Oh, I don't know. I've eaten it before. Rice is okay – even the avocado. It's more of the idea I'm eating raw fish that bothers me."

"So you don't care for ahi tuna, either?"

"Honestly, I've never wanted to try it."

He smiled.

"What have you and your friends been up to?"

"Shopping, enjoying the restaurants, trying to help Sam avoid being arrested for murdering Chef Gumm."

Drew grew quiet.

"Don't tell me you and your friends are on the investigating team with Mark."

"Not officially."

I waited before saying anything else, taking a bite of succulent teriyaki.

"I haven't talked to Eva in a while," he said. "Do they have a strong case against the Hunt boy?"

"It's strong. And honestly, all we have is his word he's innocent.

"Is he the only suspect?"

"There is another. But the police are keeping it quiet. They need more proof."

"I see. If there's any way I can help, I would be happy to."

"What we need is to find out more about what happened that night. You were there – we talked to Bill Wright and Ron Carson."

"Oh yes, we had a meeting in the back dining room. City council business."

"About rezoning issues, wasn't it? You'll have to forgive me but we have asked countless questions to find answers."

"No problem. I understand. It was probably not a good idea to meet without the other members, but I was anxious to know their thoughts on the issue."

"Do you want to sell?"

"I'm thinking about it. Offers come in occasionally but one came in recently, which is tempting. I've been thinking about making a change in my life."

"But the sale would require the inn to be rezoned."

"Yes, for condos. But if a buyer wants to continue using the inn as a hotel, a vote to rezone wouldn't be necessary."

After finishing the rest of my meal, I took a sip of tea, and placed my hand on his.

"Drew, would you be willing to help us by telling everything about the evening it happened?"

He studied my hand over his, and covered them both with his other one.

"If it will help Sam."

CHAPTER TWENTY

Our dinner at Aki lasted two hours. By the time I returned to Ingrid's, Teddy was fast asleep on my bed.

Ingrid sat in the overstuffed chair in her long fleece robe.

She motioned toward my room.

"He conked out about an hour ago."

"Sorry for the late hour. I didn't realize the time."

I took a seat on the sofa.

"The evening was productive, though. Drew and I held a lengthy conversation about what happened with Chef Gumm."

"I'm glad. Did you learn anything to help clear Sam?"

"Drew said he can prove Gumm was alive after Sam left the parking lot."

"Good! What are you going to do now?"

I stretched.

"Get a good night's sleep. Tomorrow I'll find a way to talk to Quincy and get his side of what happened."

"He usually makes his rounds early morning around eight."

"Does he deliver every morning?"

She nodded.

"The chefs pride themselves on fresh produce."

I rose from the sofa and rubbed the small of my back.

"I'm going to bed. Thanks so much for watching Teddy."

"I'm going to turn in, too. Teddy is like a grandbaby, only I don't have to change his diapers."

We chuckled.

"Sam and Claire will give you grandchildren soon enough."

A cloud covered her face.

"*If* Sam is vindicated."

"I'm praying he will be. Goodnight, my friend."

"'Night, Jillian. Thanks for all you're doing."

I gave her a hug.

Back in my room, I undressed in the dark so I wouldn't wake Teddy. A bath could wait until morning.

I looked out the window over the lake, calm and peaceful.

What about the lives of Drew, Eva, and Sam? Would peace come to them?

Drew was tired of his situation.

Eva was grieving for her husband.

And Sam was sitting on a time bomb as a prime suspect for murder.

As I tried to sleep, my thoughts turned to Quincy Morgan.

Here was a young man with not much hope of ever getting ahead. Even if Hunt's farm joined the Exchange, would it mean much of an adjustment in pay?

Up until tonight we couldn't prove, without a shadow of a doubt, that Quincy was at the scene during the time of the murder.

It was time to confront him. With The Lord's help, maybe I could convince him to tell the truth.

After I prayed, I embraced sweet sleep.

"Up and at 'em, Teddy."

He raised his head, slowly stood, and stretched out his front paws.

"By the looks of all this sunshine outside, I'd say it was going to be a good day. What do you think?"

"Woof!"

"Just as I thought. You don't really understand everything I say, do you?"

Teddy whined, long and low.

Perhaps he responded the way he did from the tone of my voice. I couldn't be sure.

"We're going to try to catch Quincy this morning. Let's get you ready for your walk."

"Woof, woof!"

Now there was a word he understood perfectly.

Ingrid left coffee and sticky buns for breakfast.

I liked this woman.

With Teddy secured on his red rhinestone leash the two of us trudged toward the parking lot at the inn, stopping several times for him to sniff.

I prayed again for perfect timing.

And there it was! Quincy's truck we'd seen him driving when he'd passed by our cafe the other day.

Thank you, Lord.

The kitchen door was held open by a sack of potatoes.

I peered in to see if Quincy was around.

"Can I help you, Mrs. Bradley?" It was Chef Pratt.

"Is Quincy here?"

"Yeah, he's inside the truck getting the next load."

"Thanks, Chef Pratt."

Calling him by his title seemed to make him smile.

Teddy raced to the truck, as if he knew exactly what to do.

I loved this dog.

Quincy poked his head out the back of the truck. He held a box full of mixed greens.

"Hey, Mrs. Bradley. Hello, Teddy."

I hung my head and spoke in the saddest voice I could muster.

"Hi, Quincy."

He set the greens on the floor of the truck and stepped down to the pavement.

Teddy pawed Quincy's legs, as if asking to be held.

"Can I hold him?"

I nodded, and sighed.

"Let's get in the shade," Quincy said. "Dogs can get hot out in the sun."

"Good idea, thanks."

We moved closer to a tree and sat on the ledge of the flowerbed.

"I hope I'm not taking up your work time," I said.

"No. It's okay. I can take a break. You seem down. What's the trouble?"

I shook my head, then looked him straight in the eye.

"Chief Taylor has to arrest Sam for murdering Chef Gumm."

Quincy was quiet.

"There doesn't seem to be any other choice given the circumstances. My heart breaks for him...and Claire."

"I didn't know you knew them."

"Oh yes. I was at their wedding. We've been friends for a long time."

"Can they prove he did it?"

"The evidence is circumstantial but Sam had strong enough motive, and Chef Pratt saw Sam near the kitchen when the chef was killed."

I managed a few more tears.

Teddy cocked his head and whined.

Good dog.

"Poor Claire," I continued. "Her husband will go to prison for the rest of his life. His father will be devastated."

I waited for the message to sink in.

"But..." I sniffed. "If Sam did kill him, he should be punished. I mean, it wouldn't be fair to Eva for him to go free. Wouldn't you agree?"

I wiped my eyes.

Quincy handed Teddy to me.

"I need to get back to unloading the truck. Don't worry, Mrs. Bradley. Things will work out for Sam."

I nodded and sniffed again.

"I hope so, Quincy. Thanks for letting me share."

"No problem. No problem at all."

With my plan set in motion, I waited until Quincy was in the kitchen, then texted Ann.

"I'm in the parking lot. Quincy is doing a delivery. You and Nicole keep an eye on him and tell me what he does."

Teddy and I continued our walk around the premises giving them time to observe Quincy's movements.

Five minutes later Ann called.

"He just closed the back of the truck. Now he's opening the door and getting in. Looks like he's calling someone. He has the phone to his ear."

"Good."

"Okay, he started the engine and is driving away. What's going on, Jillian?"

"Can you and Nicole meet me out front? We'll go for coffee and I'll explain."

"We'll be finished in a minute."

Waiting was the hard part. But if what I suspected was true, Quincy had only two choices – cut and run, or stay, and tell Chief Taylor what really happened.

It was all over by the following afternoon. Quincy turned himself in at the police station to Chief Taylor.

Sam was exonerated. Drew was no longer a suspect.

On our final night in Lake Placid, in honor of Sam, Ingrid invited a group of us over for a celebration dinner.

Guests included Sam and Claire, Drew and Eva, Ann and Nicole, Chief Taylor, and a surprise guest, John Peterson.

Ingrid served a delicious buffet of enchiladas, beans, Spanish rice, tortillas and flan for dessert.

. Toward the end of dinner, Claire beamed at Sam.

"I can't believe it's over," she said.

"Thanks to Quincy." He gave her a peck on the cheek.

"And let's not forget Jillian and her friends." Chief Taylor raised his glass to me. "That was quite a risk you took with Quincy, ma'am."

"Don't call me ma'am."

We all chuckled.

"It's true, Chief. He could have harmed me."

"Or killed you, Jillian." Drew shook his head.

"How did you know it was Quincy?" John asked.

I set my plate aside.

"I didn't. Not until Drew told me his side of the story."

He held up his hand.

"Let me tell it."

Eva gave a faint smile, probably glad she still had her brother.

"I met with a couple of council members in the private dining room near the kitchen to find out the status of a rezoning issue. Offers have been made to buy the inn."

He looked at Eva, who seemed surprised at his words.

"After the meeting was over, I heard a noise in the kitchen. Evidently Chef Gumm was listening the whole time, and overheard plans to sell."

Teddy stretched out on the carpet next to Fritz.

"What happened?" Eva asked.

"He was angry and confronted me. When he said he would never allow Eva to support the sale, I was furious and called him a fool."

"And that was the last time you saw him?" Nicole asked.

He nodded as I took up the story.

"Earlier in the evening, Quincy met with Gumm to discuss the dissatisfaction he had with the quality and prices of produce."

"There was nothing wrong with it," Sam said.

"As Quincy was leaving, Sam heard Gumm say, 'You've had your last chance."

"Right. Then I confronted Chef Gumm, we stepped outside, and he hit me."

"Quincy observed Sam and Gumm in the parking lot from behind the dumpster – curious as to what was happening to his friend."

Ann spoke.

"So Quincy decides to confront Gumm because he's defending Sam."

Chief Taylor nodded.

"He told us as much. Before he did, he heard Drew arguing with him, so Quincy waited. When Drew went back to the dining room to clear away the meeting, Quincy entered the kitchen, found the chef sitting at his desk, and stabbed him."

Eva buried her head in her hands.

"I'm sorry. This is difficult, but I want to know what happened. Go on, Mark."

"After he put the body far inside the walk in freezer and covered it with a tarp, he locked the freezer door, left the key in the lock, and turned off the lights."

Drew held up his hand again.

"When I took the glasses from the meeting into the kitchen, I assumed Gumm was gone. I thought he'd forgotten to take the freezer key to the front desk so I took it in for him."

"And when you did," John said, "I later suspected you'd killed him and told Ann and Nicole."

"Talk about the way rumors get started." Ingrid brought in a tray of coffee.

Eva looked thoughtful.

"If only Gumby treated people better, he might still be alive. I wish...."

Chief Taylor set his coffee aside and rose from his chair.

"I'd better see Eva home. This evening has been hard for her. Ingrid, thanks for your hospitality. The enchiladas were delicious."

"Goodnight, Eva. Get some rest."

Eva nodded and said goodbye to everyone.

"Come along, Fritz," the chief said.

Fritz obeyed.

Teddy popped up his head, got up, and followed them to the door.

"Stay, Teddy," I commanded.

He sat obediently.

John stood as Eva and the chief left.

"I should be leaving, too. Thanks for inviting me, Ingrid."

He gave her a peck on the cheek.

"It was good to have you, John. You're always welcome."

"Goodnight, ladies, Sam."

"See you at the inn," Claire said.

"Sam, are you ready to go home?"

"More than ready, sweetheart. I'll finally be able to get a good night's sleep."

Claire turned to my friends and me.

"We owe you everything. Thanks for saving Sam's life."

They hugged us.

It was time for us to go home, too.

We would be leaving with wonderful memories of beautiful displays of fall color, Mirror Lake set against the Adirondacks, and church bells ringing.

But most of all I would carry home the satisfaction of helping Quincy accept the consequences of his actions and by doing so, save the life of his friend.

EPILOGUE

Leaving Mirror Lake's idyllic setting was bittersweet. The place was incredibly beautiful in the fall. I would miss the fog along the shoreline and the church bells.

I could only imagine how spectacular the snow-covered inn would look in wintertime.

Thoughts of snow led to Drew. From our trip up the ski lift, it was obvious how much he loved skiing.

He never said goodbye.

Perhaps it was for the best. I wasn't ready for more change in my life in the romance department. Instead, my friends would be the ones I looked to for support.

Eva did pay a visit before I left.

"Where's Fritz?" I asked.

"Mark has him at his house. Just for now."

I smiled.

She blushed.

"Thank you again for helping me bringing closure to my husband's death. It means a great deal."

We hugged each other goodbye.

"Good luck with Mark," I said.

Unable to hide a smile, I knew she cared for him.

"Safe trip home, Jillian. I hope you'll visit again, even though we *are* selling the inn."

"So you and Drew decided to sell."

"It was for the best. The ski school offered him a job as head instructor. He didn't hesitate."

"I'm so happy for him – it's absolutely perfect. Wish him well for me, will you?"

She nodded.

"He did like you. But I think he wanted a new start with *everything*."

"I can't blame him. Thanks for coming to say goodbye."

Ingrid was busy in the bathroom giving Teddy a bath. It looked like he was going for a swim, only with bubbles.

"I couldn't let him go home without looking his best." She rinsed him off, squeezed out the water from his fur, and gathered him in a towel.

"He did enjoy those walks along the lake."

"Woof!" he barked.

"No more w.a.l.k.s. until we reach home, sweet dog. Ann and Nicole are due any minute."

Ingrid used a hair dryer to get him ready to travel. She held him as I put my bags inside the SUV. With one last kiss and a hug for Teddy, she handed him to me.

"Thanks for everything, Ingrid."

"You must come back some spring when the garden is at its peak."

"That would be a marvelous trip, but why don't you send pictures until we can return?"

"I will." She waved as we pulled away.

After leaving Lake Placid, away from Eva and all the others, I shared details Chief Taylor told me.

"I found out more about what provoked Quincy to stab Chef Gumm."

"Other than him probably not going with the exchange?" Ann asked.

"Or the way he treated him?" Nicole added.

"Are you ready for this?" I asked.

"It was Chef Gumm who smothered Drew and Eva's mother and tossed her body out the window."

Ann and Nicole gasped!

"But why did he kill their mother?" Ann asked. "Why take such drastic measure?"

"Drew once told me Mrs. Olson wanted to fire Gumm. She believed he was no good."

"Looks like she was right. He made certain he wasn't fired." Nicole said. "How did the chief discover the gruesome details?"

"After he was arrested, during the interrogation, Quincy told him he knew it was Gumm the whole time. A friend of his worked at the home."

"Someone was a witness?" Ann asked. "Why didn't they come forward?"

"Quincy said people were terrified of Gumm. They were afraid he'd kill them too."

"So Quincy must have told his friend he didn't have to worry about repercussion since Gumm was dead." Ann quickly summed up the situation.

"Exactly. After he was arrested, Quincy gave the name to Chief Taylor."

"Case closed. Does Eva know?" Nicole asked.

"No, but Drew does. Chief Taylor thought it best for Eva to believe her mother suffered from Alzheimer's."

"I think he's right," Ann said.

"Coupled with the way Gumm treated him and Sam, and remembering he killed Mrs. Olson, he overheard Gumm telling Drew he'd never let Eva sell her part of the inn, Quincy murdered him."

We rode in silence, each contemplating the happenings of the previous few days, the rest of the way to Albany's airport.

After arriving home in Clover Hills, Cecilia surprised me with pleasant news. She and Walter were expecting again!

It was good to be home, especially with a new baby on the way. I settled into my cozy cottage and made a cup of tea to enjoy while I unpacked.

As I finished putting the suitcase in the top of the closet, I wondered what my next trip would be. I didn't have immediate plans, but things could change.

A little weary, I stuffed my phone into my pocket and went into the living room to check emails, relax, and finish my tea.

There was a text from a somewhat familiar last name. *Fontaine*. This must be one of Vincent's sons!

I sat straight then read the text aloud:
Dear Jillian,

My brother Eric and I received word from our father regarding how much your visit to Costa Rica meant to him. He doesn't communicate often. Since Dad is quite fond of you, we believe you should be aware of his condition. He's too proud to tell you himself for fear of pity.

We only recently learned Dad is undergoing tests for CFS – Chronic fatigue syndrome. He's under the care of a great doctor. The bad news is Dad's tenure at the research facility will end soon. He simply cannot keep up with his research. We hope this helps explain his situation.

My brother and I fully intend to see that he receives the best of care. We're in hopes that a cure will soon be found.

Best regards,
Vince Fontaine, Jr.

I set the phone on the coffee table.

The message explained everything – Vincent's' reticence to tell me about his condition, the obvious retraction of a marriage proposal, and why he made no attempt to contact me.

I cried. *Lord, what can I do?* My heart was broken for this wonderful man of whom I was so fond.

Teddy crawled into my lap to comfort me.

I held him close.

How awful for Vincent—he was my age! For him, losing his job doing research on his beloved orchids must be devastating.

And yet, Vincent could rest in the fact that his research techniques helped save many endangered species.

How I'd love to tell him. But I couldn't because he was too proud and practical.

There was nothing I could do to reach out and support him that wouldn't cause more pain.

Letting him go, I bowed my head, and thanked the Lord Vincent's sons would take care of him.

Just as I opened my eyes, Teddy pricked up his ears at the sound of someone outside the door, and jumped down. After a brief knock, my godson D.J. bounded inside followed by Cecilia, his mother and my dear friend.

Teddy yipped excitedly and went to his toy basket searching for his blue pig.

I knew he wanted to play fetch.

"Gigi!" D.J. ran into my arms and hugged my neck.

This was the cutest little boy I'd ever known.

He had my heart.

That night I slept a peaceful sleep.

What would tomorrow bring?

The End

If you enjoyed **"Murder at Mirror Lake,"** please leave a review on your favorite reading site.

Thank you!

Go Jillian and Teddy!

Also by Nancy Jill Thames

Murder in Half Moon Bay
Book 1

The Ghost Orchid Murder
Book 2

From the Clutches of Evil
Book 3

The Mark of Eden
Book 4

Pacific Beach
Book 5

Waiting for Santa
Book 6

The Ruby of Siam
Book 7

The Long Trip Home
Book 8

Coming 2015!

MURDER
AT
THE EMPRESS HOTEL

A Jillian Bradley
Mystery

BOOK 10

NANCY JILL THAMES

MURDER
AT
THE EMPRESS HOTEL

Set in the beautiful city of Victoria on Vancouver Island, a bitter conflict over fishing rights and the love of one woman turns deadly with the murder of a young attorney, drawing Jillian and Teddy into yet another exciting adventure.

ABOUT THE AUTHOR

Nancy Jill Thames was born to write mysteries. From her early days as the neighborhood storyteller to the Amazon Author Watch Bestseller List, she has always had a vivid imagination and loves to solve problems – perfect for plotting whodunits.

In 2010, Nancy Jill published her first mystery *Murder in Half Moon Bay*, introducing her well-loved protagonist Jillian Bradley, and clue-sniffing Yorkie, "Teddy."

When she isn't plotting Jillian's next perilous adventure, Nancy Jill travels between Texas and California finding new ways to spoil her grandchildren, playing classical favorites on her baby grand or having afternoon tea with friends.

She is a member of Leander Writers' Guild, American Christian Fiction Writers (ACFW CenTex Chapter), and Central Texas Authors.

To learn more about Nancy Jill, visit
http://www.nancyjillthames.com or
contact her at jillthames@gmail.com.

17093090R00133

Made in the USA
San Bernardino, CA
30 November 2014